Coarse Witchcraft 2

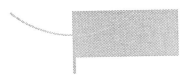

Rupert Percy & Gabrielle Sidonie

Carry On Crafting

First published in Great Britain by ignotus press 2004

BCM-Writer, London WC1N 3XX
© Rupert Percy & Gabrielle Sidonie 2004

British Library Cataloguing in Publication Data
ISBN: 1 903768 28 4

Printed in Great Britain by A2 Reprographics
Set in Baskerville Old Face 11pt

Introduction: Carry On Crafting

Carry On Crafting is the second in the *Coarse Witchcraft* series and chronicles the activities of an Old Craft coven, based in the South of England. Whereas the differences between the various witchcraft Traditions grow wider with each passing year, it has been gratifying to know that those with a little more experience under their cords have been able to see the funny side of the book — even to giving *Coarse Witchcraft: Craft Working* a 5-star rating on amazon. com!

Dedicated to all those Crafters who
believe that reverence should be tempered
with mirth and merriment.

Prologue

Since the publication of *Coarse Witchcraft: Craft Working*, the Coven has undergone several changes. The major difference is, that much to Granny's chagrin, Adam and Pris have refused to attend any more of her arranged Circle workings involving strangers, no matter how tantalising the prospect of gossip. Once their experiences had been committed to print, they decided that never mind the lunatic performances of the hosts, their *own* credibility was being seriously compromised by being seen to be taking part in such travesties of Craft.

But the best laid plans of mice and witches ...

By and large the Coven remains pretty much the same, although our working numbers are down to a handful due to the loss of Helena, our mad medium, who ran off with a lesbian lover, and the absence of our son and daughter, Richard and Philly, being away at College. Madeleine and Robert are still staunch members although Robert's job has taken them abroad for three years. Gordon still puts in an appearance but he's courting a girl from the next village, so he spends most of his time over there, once he's finished at the stables. We have to let them all go ... so that eventually they come back.

Besides myself and my wife, Gabrielle, that leaves Pris and Adam, Gerry and Guy (who run Castor & Pollux, the local occult shop) and, of course, Granny, who is itching to interfere with Gordon's relationship and draw him back into the fold: especially as the girlfriend happens to be the daughter of a Pentecostal lay-preacher. My half-brother and I are no longer on speaking terms, and the teaching coven has disbanded – much to our relief - when they realised how much work and commitment was expected from each of them.

On a more positive note, several books about what we believe (rather than what we do) have been, or are about to be written. As a result, St Thomas on the Poke is becoming the literary centre of the pagan world and never before has the kitchen table witnessed such in-depth discussions of what should, and should definitely *not*, be included in everyone's next *magnum opus*. Needless to say, there are no great secrets revealed in any of our titles but *A Witch's Treasury for Hearth & Garden* and *White Horse: Equine Magical Lore* do give a whiff of the "real stuff", as one highly re-spected occult author put it.

Rupert Percy

One impulse from a vernal wood
May teach you more of man,
Of moral evil and of good,
Than all the sages can

William Wordsworth

All Hallows

"So if I were to join in one of these witchcraft rituals, would I have to run up and down with a lighted taper in my arse, singing the *Hallelujah Chorus*?" The question was patronising and more than a little offensive, even if it wasn't on camera.

Rupert fixed the interviewer with a steely look before responding in his best, clipped public-school tone: "You could if you wanted to, old boy, but it wouldn't add anything constructive to the proceedings."

With that, he climbed into the Land Rover and drove off, leaving the television crew staring after him, open-mouthed, while the public relations girl looked as though she was about to burst into tears. I *had* warned them well in advance not to ask daft questions but obviously the media genius with the Beckham mentality had decided to busk it - and this was the result. So there they stood in the middle of a field, on a damp October morning - a complete production team, whose star performer had just buggered off! And no amount of coaxing was going to get him back.

Needless to say, it was a couple of weeks away from Hallowe'en, and this was an attempt to inject something 'topical but spooky' into the early evening *Country-Style* programme. Rupert had only agreed to take part because he'd been led to believe it related directly to his new book, *White Horse: Equine Magical Lore* and he was expecting to talk about traditional British 'horse whispering' and natural animal cures. (He can wax quite lyrical about pig oil and sulphur, which he considers to be a cure for most things. I once caught him eyeing the children speculatively when they were small and suffering from measles!) He was *not* prepared to talk about Old Craft, on or off camera, with a moron who was just trying to provoke some good television.

As we've said many times before, the problem is that the media doesn't want to portray witches as sane and rational adults with jobs and family responsibilities. They *want* weird (as opposed to *wyrd*) and will try any trick to manoeuvre their victim into doing, or saying, something stupid so the nation can snigger behind its collective hand, convinced that we're all mentally defective. Unfortunately, there are a handful of so-called magical practitioners who *will* perform this kind of stunt for five minutes of fame but they are only representative of those whose roots were grafted after the popular surge of occultism in the 1970s.

Having finally managed to sooth Rupert's affronted pride, and attempted to persuade the production crew that camping out in the greenhouse wasn't a good idea, most of the morning had gone. Judging by the amount of frantic mobile telephone activity – conspicuous in a stableyard by the discordant assortment of electronic ring-tones – they had obviously been told not to return to base without a result. For some time we amused ourselves by watching from the upstairs windows as they circled the house, trying to conceal themselves among the bushes and shrubs, waiting to pounce. The publicity girl, now thoroughly sodden, had tried banging on the door a couple of times, but Rupert was not for turning. It was going to be a long day, but the dog was keeping them on the move, and finding it all immense fun.

Periodically, someone would mooch past the kitchen window, sporting what appeared to be a dead ferret on the end of a pole. I was reliably informed by my son (who telephoned in the middle of this hiatus), that it was a microphone and part of the sound equipment, but out here in the country, you can never be quite sure. We know of one local lad who managed to sell the same dead fox to a television production team on three consecutive days, by keeping it in the freezer overnight and fluffing up the fur each morning with his mother's hair-dryer. And they say country folk are thick ... he earned £100 for that road-kill!

Anyway, Rupert refused to leave the kitchen while the media circus was still lurking about, and just as we were sitting down to an early lunch, in came Pris, spitting feathers. "I'll murder the bugger!" she kept saying, until Rupert's special blend of strong coffee laced with *Famous Grouse* worked its magical calming effect; not to mention feeding her a cheese and pickle sandwich, the size of which would have felled a healthy Rottweiler.

At first we thought poor old Adam was coming in for some flack but it was much more serious than mere marital dispute. A stranger had ridden into town and, compounding sacrilege with blasphemy, had announced to all and sundry that he came from the very same Old Craft tradition that had spawned Pris. Now we have ways and means of recognising our 'own', as is were, and this pretender was not giving out any of the signals that would have endorsed his claim.

In all honesty, Pris's old teacher was a bit of a colourful character with some most peculiar working methods - which may account for some of Pris's strange habits - but his magical approach was certainly unique. As she'd said on many occasions in response to prior bogus claims to her lineage: "He might have been a scurrilous old bugger, but he was *our* scurrilous old bugger!"

This type of claiming 'kinship' is, unfortunately, no longer a rarity, especially as the schism between contemporary Wicca and the Gardnerian-based traditions is widening all the time. Those older traditions that have formal, initiatory training and an established hierarchical system now wish to distance themselves from this eclectic free-for-all that typifies 21st century paganism, by referring to themselves as 'traditional' Craft.

For those of British Old Craft, however, the gulf between modern paganism and our ways could *never* have been reconciled. As we frequently point out, there's nothing altruistic about Old Craft, which retains its tribal mentality and does not wish to take on the responsibility for global problems that occur outside its own sphere of operations. We tend to work on the guiding and hallowed principle of looking after our own ... full stop!

All this convenient pagan colour-coding has resulted in more and more folk coming forward to claim antecedents for themselves, to which they are not entitled. As a rule they allow around five years from the death of one of these Old Souls and if no-one else appears to lay claim to the tradition, they publicly proclaim themselves to be the inheritors of the old wisdom of the dear departed. Even if the closest they've ever been is bumping into one at a pagan camp; holding a couple of telephone conversations of a pseudo-magical nature; or being involved in the same public ritual as '*the Name*'. Old Crafters are notoriously secretive and this form of *lèse-majesté* is the only thing that will bring 'em out of the woodwork to defend their corner. There's many a pretender who has been faced down by an affronted Old Crafter ... and it's not a pretty sight!

"So who is this chap?" I asked, when Pris had cooled down enough to talk coherently and wiped the smear of home-made chutney from her cheek.

"He's just taken over as relief manager of the Duck & Ferret in the next village, and called into Castor & Pollux, to introduce himself as a traditional witch. Of course Gerry kept quiet while he rattled off his pedigree but he wasted no time in getting on the phone to me to check him out once the chap was off the premises."

Gerry has elevated the art of keeping 'closeted' to an art form and will rarely give anything away about his own background, magical or personal. There are still those pagan groups who have difficulties accepting homosexuals in their midst, but this reveals more about their magical abilities than their personal prejudices. Our 'boys' are valued members of the Coven and no one can prise information out of unsuspecting customers like our Gerry.

"And there's no way he *could* be one of your erstwhile band?" said Rupert, attempting to prevent any knee-jerk reactions involving hexing, bottling or spit-roasting, or a combination of all three.

"Nope. I did my own checking. The Old Man never formally initiated the person who this chap claims initiated *him*, and I *can* prove that. It's like one of us claiming initiatory links with the New Forest lot simply because we live within spitting distance of the forest and Granny having had some spurious connection with them in days gone by. No, I got my facts right *before* I lost my temper."

"Anything we can use publicly?" I asked, knowing that some of their strange ways might raise an eyebrow or two in some circles. And some things *are* most definitely best kept hidden.

Pris fiddled with her spoon for a moment or two and then a grin started to play at the corners of her mouth. "Do you remember some years ago, when the Old Man *accidentally* revealed that bogus rite to a chap who was so desperate to join the coven, and wouldn't take 'no' for an answer? ..."

" ... Then an article subsequently appeared in a highly respected pagan magazine, claiming to be revealing a secret rite from an authentic tradition, and written by one of their revered Elders?" It pays to have a long memory.

"Yup. As you know, there were some extremely stupid, tell-tale words inserted in the chant and now this chap has claimed that knowing them *proves* he's genuine! Of course he can't reveal the whole thing, it being secret and all that ..." she laughed again. "We couldn't believe it when the rite appeared in print because it was complete and utter garbage but now it's doing the rounds as his passport to Old Craft."

"Is it the same chap who wrote the article?"

"Judging from Gerry's description I'd say not, but he's certainly picked it up from somewhere."

"So what's his name?" asked Rupert.

"He's calling himself Arthur Kinsman but he's no kinsman of *mine.*"

"Well, you know what they say, Pris," replied Rupert with a gleam in his eye. "Half a kinsman is better than none." We all burst out laughing and the tension was immediately diffused but 'arfa Kinsman it would remain.

Although we turned it into a joke amongst ourselves, kinship is something that genuine practitioners do take *very* seriously, although the rites and oaths they take to cement those bonds have long been the source of mockery (i.e. the Freemasons) or fear (Old Craft and the Magical Orders). Because of the symbolic threat implied by certain aspects of the rites, it is automatically assumed by outsiders to mean death should the oath be broken, or if an initiate attempts to leave the group. And because these warnings are couched in purple prose, the implications can appear extremely alarming, if not down-right frightening to the inexperienced. This may have been necessary when occult practice was deemed heretical and carried its own death penalty but in today's magical circles the implications are much more subtle.

Perhaps this is best described by Uncle Aleister himself, who explained that any oath taken within an esoteric order is deemed sacred and, because magical punishment always fits the crime, it is inadvisable to betray the group, or any individual fellow member, without expecting some kick-back. The understanding of this is all part of the Initiatory experience but the esoteric meaning is much more significant.

When the Initiate takes the oath, it is to *themselves* as well as to the group, and usually involves making certain statements on, or by the deity, in which they believe. Subsequently, anyone breaking such an oath is blaspheming only themselves and "having switched on the current of disloyalty [he] would have found disloyalty damaging him again and again until he had succeeded in destroying himself."

Spooky stuff, I agree, but it *is* All Hallows and magical law has a way of running its own course. Those who publicly blaspheme it by claiming spurious connections to that which they have no entitlement are insulting those who *do* keep the faith; what they don't realise is they also risk the "most frightful dangers to life, liberty and reason" that they are drawing down upon *themselves*. The repercussions are as *natural* as a lightning strike and this is probably the complex origin of the modern, dumbed-down version of the 'law of three-fold return'.

A couple of days later, the four of us were sitting around talking about our own All Hallows rite and how we were going to observe it. It's always a source of mirth for us when so-called pagans talk about 'celebrating' Samhain, since death and the honouring of the ancestors is hardly a *celebratory* occasion. After all, would any sane adult think of 'celebrating' the anniversary of September 11th or Remembrance Day with games and frivolity?

Nevertheless, it is always a problem when running a working coven to try and think of something different to try that will continually push the boundaries of our own abilities. It also magically challenges everyone in the group when there is some ultimate goal to aim for, and in our own Coven we have always tried to maintain a tangible contact with the shades of previous generations of witches, from whom we draw our inspiration and understanding.

We were in the middle of our discussion when Granny turned up and I could hardly leaving her standing on the doorstep, when the rest of us were sitting cosy and warm around the coffee pot. So I invited her in, despite Rupert banning her from the house on account of her rather distinctive and pungent personal odour.

In all fairness, this has improved quite dramatically since the demise of her rather decrepit sheepdog and the kidnapping of her vile old tomcat; the latter being lured away for a couple of days and surgically altered by a well-meaning cat charity. We suspect the neighbours finally got fed up with it spraying in their rather expensive Amdega conservatory, and under the pretence of it being a stray, handed it over for a clandestine de-balling! Granny wasn't best pleased but even with all her magical skills it wasn't possible to retrieve the severed testicles from the vet's incinerator.

Rupert scowled meaningfully and I sat her down at the furthest point from the Aga, just in case she started to ferment in the heat. Without any preamble she pressed home her attack in her usual forthright matter. "What are you going to do about this Kinsman fella?"

"Nothing." Rupert has always resented the way his own father was coerced into marrying Granny Jay's daughter, and so allows her no quarter when it comes to Coven business. It had long since ceased to surprise us as to how Granny always managed to be one step ahead of any gossip or drama unfolding.

"Young Pris can't be expected to defend her own corner without some sort of back up," she continued. 'Young' Pris managed to look both innocent and amused, while Adam was developing his customary 'rabbit faces stoat' expression that characterises his reaction to any close proximity to Granny. Both chose to remain silent and let battle commence.

"She won't have to," said Rupert stiffly, "but nothing will be gained by going off half-cocked. Sooner of later he'll make a fool of himself – they always do."

"Ay, they do as that," said Granny, taking a hefty slug of overly sweetened tea. "Do you remember that little madam who claimed to have inherited my teaching? Gave her the shock of her life when she discovered I wasn't dead and that I was standing right behind her ... and had heard *every* word."

There are those who might be forgiven for thinking Granny *was* dead on the grounds that nothing living could smell that bad, but we let it pass. The real villain of the piece in the odour stakes is the large Bagot goat she allows to walk in and out of the cottage as it chooses. As a result, the stench of billy-goat pervades everything, but Granny remains oblivious to her neighbours jostling for an up-wind position whenever conversation is unavoidable.

Her bright blue eyes watched Rupert closely from under her battered waxed hat. "What are you going to do about Gordon?"

"Nothing." As far as Rupert's concerned, Granny surrendered her authority when she decided to step down as Dame, and so refuses to accept any interference despite her still being an argumentative, meddlesome old crone. Nevertheless, we now knew the real reason behind her visit.

"The boy will come to harm, if he's left to his own devices. He's besotted with that girl. The parents are making out they don't mind him following the Old Ways but as soon as the ring's on her finger it will be a different kettle of fish all together, you mark my words! I've heard it said that she's been told 'you just get him wed, my girl, your father will see to his spiritual needs'."

We all perked up over this bit of news and wondered who

would be delegated to magically sock it to the Holy Rollers but Rupert had other ideas. "If that's the Path he *wants* to follow, we can't stop him. I agree with you that it would be a tragic waste but we don't have the right to interfere ... even if we personally believe him to be misguided, he must make his own choice."

Granny looked mutinous and the words "over my dead body" hung unspoken in the air but she swallowed her chagrin and joined in the All Hallows discussion. None of us were fooled for a moment but this kind of moral dilemma is a double-edged sword and the rest of us could identify with both Rupert and Granny, on either side of the argument. On the other hand, this particularly virulent brand of evangelism with its spiritual healing and 'speaking in tongues' is highly contagious and none of us (including Rupert) were convinced by Granny's seemingly demure acceptance.

To throw a smoke-screen over the subject, she started with one of her stories.

"We can *all* make mistakes over inaction," she said meaningfully. "During the last war, our coven had taken a battering and was magically under-manned, but they were troubled times and the All Hallows rite needed to be observed. One cold November night a small group of us gathered in the woods and the working area was prepared in the Old Way, and although I had my doubts about one of the group, I said nothing. The particular rite we were working was a familiar one for most of us, and previous generations had probably felt much the same stirrings around their backs, as the Old Words rose and fell in its rhythmic chant.

"As we slowly began to circle together, there was an air of expectancy. Nothing was spoken, and not even a meaningful glance passed between us, but we all knew 'something' was brewing. The air almost crackled with magic. At the appropriate time, the chanting stopped, and each stood or knelt, gazing into the cauldron that now seemed huge enough to swallow the world."

Granny can be quite poetic when talking about the old days and we hung on every word, even though we knew there would be a sting in the tail. "From the corner of my eye, I noticed a shadowy, cowled figure walking the perimeter of our circle. It was tall and graceful, and in no way threatening; no blood-splattered spectre as we might have expected, given the times in which we were living. Everyone held their breath, for this was the moment we had worked so hard towards for such a long time. I sensed the recognition, and though I did not know exactly which of our ancestors had answered the call, I was certain that it was one who was very familiar with the old rite. Stealing a sideways glance, I saw that the others were also awe-struck by its closeness. Time stood still, and we experienced that thrill of enjoying a mutually magical moment, and my mind was in a whirl. Could we hold the contact – should we interact with our visitor? Not least of all I thought: 'What the hell do we do now!'

"We were saved (if that's the right way of putting it) from making any decision about how to carry on, because suddenly the moment was shattered by the woman, whose place that night I'd previously doubted, leaping to her feet. She whirled round and without further thought, soundly banished the Wise One from our midst. Without thanks or warning, the poor soul was literarily hurled into nothingness, to vanish into the night.

"The smug creature beamed at us saying, 'Well, that showed the bugger!' and for all the world I think she was expecting to be congratulated. I was too disorientated and angry to speak, but others asked what on earth she thought she was doing? She explained in a patronising tone, that didn't we know we should be careful about beings encountered on the other planes? She did not feel that it had been invited, so she had banished it as soon as she saw it! Which begs the question of how much she ever understood about what we were about.

"The gathering was closed down in a sombre tone, and a serious discussion followed. The outcome being that the woman was asked to leave the group, her offence to the ancestors being so great as to leave us all feeling guilty. As Dame of the group, I felt that I had failed; both in having said nothing about my doubts over her ability, and in my protection of those who had gone before us. To this day, I have never again made such a contact during any group working.

"For me, hard lessons were learned that night, and the hardest one was in accepting that we cannot keep people as members of a coven simply on the basis of friendship.

I had had my doubts about her understanding on many occasions, but out of a desire to remain friends with the member who had introduced her, I hadn't had the common sense to suggest that she may not be working in total harmony with us. It can be all too easy to lose friends and incur criticism when we undertake to walk the path of the Man or Dame. Many people have an overwhelming desire to hold those titles, but how many are truly worthy of them?"

Picking up her mug, she fixed Rupert with a pointed stare over the china rim. A muscle twitched at the corner of his mouth but he decided not to respond to her goading. This issue was not going to go away and while Gordon was perfectly free to make his own decisions, there was still the underlying concern about what he might reveal about the Coven *if* he were to fall completely under the spell of the Pentecostals.

All Hallows marks the end of the Old Year and from now until the Winter Solstice is a period of Nature marking time The constellation of Orion is visible again in the east, after his sojourn in the southern hemisphere. The hunter has returned to watch over his sleeping consort until the spring; when she awakes he will slip below the horizon until he is recalled again in time for the Hunter's Moon. For us as a working group, this is a time of extremely potent magical energy and the rites we perform as the old year slips towards the new, are the ones that will take 12 moons to come to fruition.

Winter Solstice

It never ceases to amaze me how pre-occupied the pagan community at large becomes over other people's Traditions. Since the publication of the first *Coarse Witchcraft*, we find the Coven being discussed and speculated over in numerous Internet chat-rooms. Complete strangers have apparently tried to find out who we are, and where we live, and each little nugget of information is posted up in an attempt to give the poster more occult-cred than the rest.

Guy and Gerry have been forced to replace those tell-tale white sofas in Castor & Pollux in order to throw people off the scent – although they do sell our books in the shop. There have been debates over whether we are hereditary (we've *never* said we were); whether we are a channel for more sinister purposes (interesting but most certainly inaccurate); and whether we actually exist at all (oh, we do, we most assuredly do!).

Under the guise of some idiotic 'net-name' – which usually goes through the entire Celtic pantheon with depressing regularity, or something equally bizarre - like Gwenfrewi Tanglepussy – the armchair pagans exercise their right to pontificate and disseminate their views on *our* authenticity and working methods. Our son, Richard, who keeps us informed about the surfing shenanigans, will often reveal himself as a member of the Coven and offer to answer any of their more specific questions. Having suddenly manifested in their midst, however, he usually finds himself alone in the echoing vaults of cyber-space! Personally, the rest of us can't be bothered, although on a tip-off from Richard, Adam will often appear as a 'demon king' in one of the chat-rooms and stir up trouble just for the sheer hell of it – until he's kicked out.

The dictionary definition of a witch is one regarded as having supernatural or magical power and knowledge, but I'd rather go along with our old friend, the late Evan John Jones's often-quoted view: "If one who claims to be a witch can perform the tasks of witchcraft, i.e. summon the spirits and they come, can divine with rod, fingers and birds. If they can also claim the right to the omens and have them; have the power to call, heal and curse and above all, can tell the maze and cross the Lethe, then you have a witch."

For us, we also take Hotspur's stance in *Henry IV* when Glendower boasts: *"I can call spirits from the vasty deep,"* and Hotspur replies, *"Why so can I, or so can any man; But will they come, when you do call for them?"* In other words, we're really not that interested in what other people claim for themselves, except when they bring their false claims onto our turf and attempt to use them to gain access to our Coven. Call your spirits by all means, but we will demand a personal introduction.

We finally got to meet 'arfa Kinsman through an unexpected twist of fate, which was to trigger some old, and not very pleasant memories all the way around. In the winter, one of our fields is set aside for the annual point-to-point meetings, which generally start in the New Year, with the proceeds going to the upkeep of the local hunt's hounds and horses. Rupert used to ride in the races but age *has* wearied him, and he now prefers to put our son's horses through their paces, and act as a fence judge on race days. The manager of the Duck & Ferret organises the beer tent.

He was busy rubbing down one of the horses after riding out, when a shiny 4x4 pulled into the yard and out climbed a stranger, advancing on him with an outstretched hand.

"Hello there, Rupert," he greeted. "I'd been hoping to run into you around the village but haven't bumped into you or your good lady in order to talk about the bar for the point-to-point meeting. Still, nothing like bearding the lion in his den, eh?"

The bearded lion managed to out-fumble the stranger and, not having a clue who this hail-fellow-well-met chappie was, avoided shaking his hand. "Quite ... erm ... Not my area of responsibility, so I'm afraid you've come to the wrong person."

"Well, yes, I realise that but I'm a great friend of Jackie Pratt," continued the beaming stranger. "She told me to look you up if I was ever in the area. Wonderful little witch, is our Jackie."

Rupert was feeling totally bemused by this quick shift from beer tents to besoms, until Pris, unable to control her curiosity any longer, sidled up and enlightened him. "The pustuler postulant!" she hissed in his ear, referring to the named person's unfortunate skin complaint.

If Kinsman (for that's who it was) noticed the hardening of Rupert's expression, he gave no indication and turned his beaming attention on Pris who had, fortunately for us all, already recognised him from Gerry's description. "And you must be Pris. Jackie's told me how you always used to ride together. In fact, she's told me lots of stories about you all."

"I bet she has," retorted Pris, as Rupert hastily excused himself and disappeared into the house. "What's she doing with herself, these days?"

"Oh, you know ..."

"No, I *don't* know. Suppose you tell me?"

"Jackie told me all about the Coven," he replied, lowering his voice, as if frightened of the horses overhearing. "I'd just like a piece of the action. I went into that occult shop in the town, but the couple of daisies running it wouldn't know a besom from a burin. I mean the local pagan scene hardly stretches the old magical reflexes, does it?"

"I wouldn't know," she answered. "I don't have a lot to do with it."

"Oh, *come on!*" There was a hint of aggressiveness in the tone but Pris cut him short. "If you'll excuse me, we are very busy."

She had no intention of engaging in a verbal brawl in the stable yard and quickly followed Rupert's exit into the house. We always prefer to bide our time.

"Was it something you said?" asked Rupert, pouring her a coffee, to the sound of a 4x4 burning rubber across the cobbles.

"No. I don't have all my facts yet in order to challenge his claims because Kirsten hasn't got back to me. It's the fact that Pratt-face is somehow involved with him that freaks me out. By the gods, I loath that woman. She caused so much trouble ..."

"And is still doing so, by all accounts," I added, having been watching the goings-on from the safety of the kitchen window and trying to avoid falling over the dog, whose purpose in life seems to be focussed solely on getting in the way.

It's a funny thing, but in Craft it seems as though things that some folk would prefer to remain firmly besomed under the carpet, have an embarrassing habit of eventually rising to the surface. Nowadays, there is nothing that people such as 'arfa Kinsman like doing, more than 'name-dropping', but when Jackie Pratt's name had popped into the conversation, old and unwelcome memories had begun to stir in all our minds.

Jackie Pratt. The 'pustular postulant' and erstwhile competition rival of Pris's West Country schooldays, who had spotted her riding one of our horses at a local event while on holiday many years later, and assumed, quite wrongly, that Pris worked for us. She'd asked around and discovered that not only was the family one of the largest landowners in the area, but that we were well-known for our Old Craft associations. It was certainly a heady combination and it wasn't too long before Jackie Pratt was hanging around the yard whenever Pris appeared, and badgering Rupert to let her help with the horses, or talk to her about his Craft interests. As it happened, Rupert had taken an instant dislike to her and wasn't about to let her near either.

It wasn't until we were sitting together having coffee one morning, that Pris finally came clean about what had been going on in our midst for some months. It seemed that the Craft 'scene' had a new heiress to the throne, a new witch-queen – large in mouth and bosom, and generous to a fault with her affections (if the sly winks and bawdy comments made by the lads during one of Adam's rollicking rugby supporters trip, were anything to go by.)

"Adam's second-hand description rang a bell but the tintinnabulation wouldn't allow me to 'name that tune'. A couple of days after I had ridden Max in the show, I bumped into her in town, quite by chance. A complete stranger suddenly enveloped me in an alarming bear hug and exclaimed (to my horror), that she knew me of old. Perhaps the riding hat in my car had triggered her memory, but it soon transpired that as 'girls' we used to compete in the same local Pony Club events. Without further ado, she was soon waxing lyrical about her standing as head-girl in a prestigious yard, which was nothing less than impressive, considering that some of the best names in show-jumping were there.

"Having finally made a bolt for it, I remembered that I *did* know who she was, and the memory was not a happy one. As you know, when you do the Pony Club circuit, you get to see the same horseboxes, and the same people over and over again. I now clearly recalled the shabby old box, with a badly turned-out crew and, without putting too finer point on it, most of the competitors had raised an eyebrow over the condition of the ponies as well.

"For my part, I was a keen 15-year old intent on a career working with horses and I'd been up since the crack of dawn, plaiting manes and tails. Getting togged up in my best jacket, tack polished to perfection, I was feeling pretty confident that I was in with a good chance of being in the ribbons. Like any competitor, my friend and I started to take note of who might give us a run for our money. One figure in the collecting ring was attracting a few stares. It was one of the team from the shabby horsebox. The rider was hatless (you could be in those days), jacketless and wearing a t-shirt; the under-weight mare was clearly unhappy and things were not going well.

"Jackie Pratt was being urged to make more use of the whip and feeling desperately sorry for the pony, I edged closer, fully intent on attracting the attention of the steward. Finally with much shouting of *"Gerrrrrrron ya bugger!"* and copious use of the whip, the mare did a standing jump over the practice pole before galloping wildly back towards the entrance. Pratt-face, flushed and clearly very angry leaped off and the mare was swiftly taken out of sight behind the box. Before I could do or say anything, my number was called and it was my round.

When Jackie Pratt's number was called, the mare and rider emerged and shot straight through to the ring without a backward glance. The pair had a dismal round and what the mare didn't knock down, she either trashed or avoided, and once again the red-faced rider and pony disappeared. And not long afterwards, so did the box. Rumour had it that one of the officials had been seen talking to the man in charge – and that was the last I ever saw of them.

"Imagine my horror when I realised that this person, who was now supposedly in charge of some very expensive, and much loved competition animals, was the same bad tempered teenager who had given that poor pony a very hard time. The past has a habit of catching us out, and throughout her alleged magical training she obviously hasn't come across the old maxim – 'Know thyself'. If we can't know ourselves, its always wise to bear in mind that others might have better insights."

Since Jackie Pratt had been refused entry into the Coven and left the area in high dudgeon (but not before spreading a lot of highly malicious rumours), none of us had thought about her in years, but we were about to be reminded by more than just a bit of casual name-dropping ...

For the Coven, the Winter Solstice is a sacred time of the year and we always try to observe the rebirth of the Sun in a fitting way. An old friend of Pris's (from way back when she was a witchlet, and from those same origins that Kinsman claimed were his!) had come to visit and the plan was for them to take her to one of our working sites for an open air ritual, since she's been city-bound for many years. Meeting Kirsten off the train immediately raised some doubts as to the wisdom of the exercise because the intervening years had turned her into a fine strapping woman but (in her own words) not exactly built for speed trials.

Unfortunately, once Pris has the bit between her teeth, it's not that easy to deflect her from the path and she decided to carry on with the original plan. Being cautious types, the Coven has its gatherings in places that are not easily accessible, which usually means finding our way through woods, slithering down an embankment and crossing a fast running stream before scrambling up another bank to negotiate a tall stile. The site selected for this particular event is one favoured by Pris and Adam for more personal rituals but it also involves an additional trek across two large fields flanked by high hedges.

"Kirsten had found it hard going but it was a beautifully clear, crisp night and we were making our way back across the fields after the working," said Pris, as we sat in our usual place around the kitchen table trying to organise our own Solstice observance. "It had been a good one and all three of us were in good spirits as we left the darkness of the woods and climbed over the stile. As you know, when you're cold, tired and a little under the *Grouse*, not to mention carrying bags of robes, etc, that last walk across those fields can be a bit of a drag."

Under normal circumstances, Adam (who is a bit younger and fitter than the rest of us) goes striding ahead so that he reaches the car first, in order to get the engine running and the heater going full pelt. Pris, who hates the cold, gasps and grumbles loud enough to be heard three fields away, is determined to be back in front of a roaring fire as quickly as possible, and is never usually very far behind. On this particular night, Kirsten - whom Pris remembered as being an accomplished witch with nerves of steel - trudged slowly by her side.

"I was feeling pretty chilled out in all senses of the word. An owl began screeching and as I looked up, I noticed the stars seemed incredibly close and beautiful. Pausing to gaze at the heavens, I pointed out Cassiopia and the Great Bear to Kirsten. Getting no reply, I glanced around only to see her a fair way up the field, and going like a train. It crossed my mind that perhaps she was on a personal fitness thing again ... Adam was well out of sight, but the night was beautiful and for once I was content to meander.

"After a few minutes steady walking, the owl called again, and once more I stopped in my tracks to gaze up at the skies. The stars were putting on quite a show from one of the meteor showers (I forget which) ..."

"The Ursids," interrupted Rupert.

"Granted ... and I clearly saw the shadow of the owl as she swooped into an oak tree. I paused and marvelled at all this natural beauty and counted my blessings at having access to such a place where the night held no fears for me," Pris continued. "The last stile was in sight. I could see the car lights and Kirsten waving wildly - and I remember feeling sorry that they had to spoil such perfection with their impatience. The cattle were grazing in the next field and the air was so pure that I could smell them. The owl called again but the sound of the car horn rudely interrupted my reverie. I climbed the last stile as Adam pulled up alongside and gesticulated for me to hurry up and get into the car. What was wrong with these two? The night was perfect, the magic had been there in the woods, the owl was hunting, the stars were brilliant. Who would be in such a rush to leave it all behind? With one last glance at the stars, I pulled off my boots and got into the car.

"Two faces peered intently at me, but for a moment neither of them spoke until Adam broke the silence. 'Are you stark staring mad?' he asked. I gaped at him in astonishment as Kirsten butted in: 'Pris, that was either incredibly brave, or incredibly stupid!' As you know, it isn't often that I'm lost for words but this unexpected verbal battering threw me completely. Blankly I looked from one to the other, hoping that one of them would enlighten me as to what they were prattling on about, and was beginning to wonder what might have been in the altar wine."

In exasperation Adam had apparently slapped the steering wheel, then taking a deep breath, began to address his wife as though she were the village idiot. With exaggerated patience, he explained that as they had climbed out of the woods and into the field, he had spotted the very large and distinctive shape of Joseph, our prize Charolais bull in the corner, under the shadow of the trees. Knowing Joseph to be a temperamental animal and not wishing to attract too much attention to their presence, he resisted calling to warn the women and had, instead just got on with the job of getting up those fields as fast as he could. And who says the age of chivalry is dead?

Pris and Kristen had been too busy laughing about which of them was the most likely to fall over this particularly awkward stile to notice any bull, and it was not until Pris stopped to gaze at the stars that Kirsten had turned and noticed him. She assumed that as she lived and worked in the country, Pris would not be unduly worried about the fact that a *very* large Charolais bull was standing about four feet behind her. As she had huffed and puffed her way up the field, with occasion looks back over her shoulder, all she could do was marvel at her friend's unspoken empathy with the animal.

"With relish she described how Joseph, pale and ghostly loitering, had doggedly plodded along behind me as I toiled up the field," said Pris. "And each time I stopped to gaze, he had stopped with the same four feet between us, waiting patiently (thank the gods!) until I set off again. All this was a complete revelation to me! And to think how blissfully unaware I was of him being there. I still shudder to think what would have happened if I'd spotted him, but it's a pretty safe bet that I would not have noticed Cassiopia, and I would *not* have been the last to the car!"

It was also on the way home that night, Pris thought she recognised a familiar face peering out from the hedgerow, as the car sped past. "That looked like Granny," she said to Adam.

"Don't talk daft," he said, making no attempt to slow down. "What on earth would the old girl being doing out here at this time of night. It's miles from her place."

But it's not miles from Gordon's girlfriend's place, Pris had thought to herself as she recalled the glint in Granny's eye over the rim of her coffee mug just before All Hallows. But Kirsten was in the car and she didn't pursue the matter.

The Winter Solstice is an ancient celebratory rite although some of the other Traditions consider this tide (from now until the Vernal Equinox) to be one of the most dangerous for any active magical work. To be honest, we have always found it to be one of the best and would prefer to be outside under a clear winter sky working a rite, than waiting for the long summer nights. The Hunter is still visible in the sky and there is also an air of celebration and festivity about the season as we acknowledge the Old Lad in his role as the 'holly king'.

Candlemas

"Right! Thanks for the warning, Gerry," I said, switching off the phone. "Storm warning," I said to Pris, who glanced up from the estate agent's particulars she'd received that morning. "Rupert has just savaged one of Gerry's customers."

"What on earth was he doing in the shop?" she asked. "He normally avoids the place like the plague because of the morons he claims inhabit the place."

"He was doing Gordon's egg-run. Apparently some woman was asking for a statue of the Triple Moon Goddess, and two-dozen newly-laid eggs almost got scrambled on the spot. Before Gerry could head him off at the pass, he'd asked where she'd got *that* damned silly idea from, and she'd replied she'd read about it in a book."

According to the phone-in version, while Gerry was desperately hacking his way through a jungle of wind-chimes and vaulting over their lurcher to intervene, Rupert had asked between gritted teeth, what the hell the woman thought the 'goddess' did during the dark quarter of the moon's phase. No doubt expecting the 'perfect love' of universal paganism, the unfortunate creature was confronted by some raving egg-man wearing Wellington boots and a ratting-hat. Gerry managed to relieve him of the eggs and, with both hands free, Rupert began to remonstrate over the fantasy image of the goddess promulgated in pagan art and publishing. His parting shot had been: "You would not want to encounter the *real* goddess, *believe me!*" Which had sent a cold shiver down Gerry's back, never mind the effect on the poor woman who stood staring open-mouthed at the retreating figure.

"Not like Rupert to be so theatrical," said Pris. "He doesn't usually give *anything* away."

It's not easy to explain how we view the 'goddess' but Rupert's closing gambit wasn't far short of the mark. Old Craft is not a religion *per se* and so the focus for female energy in terms of magical working is seen as a seasonal manifestation, or abstract personification, of a potent Nature energy that influences the growing and the harvest. For us the 'goddess' would indeed be a terrible sight to behold and she is kept from mortal view by her protector and guardian, the 'god', who roams the fields and woodland ready to spring to her defence should any stray too close.

In ancient Egypt there was a temple inscription dedicated to the hunter-warrior goddess Neith at Sais which said: *"I am all that has been, that is, and that will be. No mortal has yet been able to lift the veil which covers me."* This is probably the closest we can get to describing our ways, and why we feel that the fantasy caricatures of pagan art that show young, glamorous lasses with flowing tresses is such a travesty. The 'goddess' in all her majesty is more likely to appear as Kali, rather than Nicole Kidman.

It probably also goes a long way to explain why Old Craft is more male oriented, simply because we raise 'Horned God energy' in order to connect and procreate magically with the 'Lass' *through* him. In modern Wicca, the 'Old Lad' has almost been dispensed with completely in favour of a feminine-cloned chimera that is both barren and illusionary when it comes to harnessing natural magical energies. Perhaps this is why Wicca has come to represent a purely devotional expression of the pagan ethos, which is nearer to Christianity than it is to traditional witchcraft.

Kirsten had phoned Pris after her visit and gone through the archive to check on whether 'arfa Kinsman had ever been a member of their old Order. Pris, not being very good with paperwork and accounts, had miraculously ducked out of inheriting it all when their old Magister had retired and the responsibility had fallen to Kirsten. A few days later she had pulled out a grubby folder that showed Kinsman's application to join the Order, having made all sorts of bogus claims to his antecedents – and that was ten years earlier.

"Thank the gods, the old man *never* threw anything out," said Pris, shuffling through the photocopies. "He carried out a thorough investigation at the time, and not one of Kinsman's claims held up when the right people were contacted. Look, dates, names, places ... and not one of them would authenticate his background."

"He's getting to be a real pain," I said reading through the papers. "Wherever I go, he seems to turn up. What's so interesting about us that *everyone* wants to join our Coven? After all, we're now down to just 'Three Studs and a Tart'."

This was the name our team was entered under in the local team-chasing event, and it was here that Kinsman had snuck up on me again while I was busy setting up the picnic in the back of the Land Rover. Team-chasing is one of those rural past-times that the Health & Safety brigade haven't yet managed to interfere with. Rupert, Gordon, Richard and Pris were over with the horses, champing at the bit and waiting for their turn over the jumps, while Adam and Philly were in the beer tent keeping out of the way in case they were roped in for something.

Then they were off, riding against the clock, with only the times of the first three in the team counting. One Stud and the Tart took the fences with ease, but the other Two Studs collided and Rupert was pitched into the gorse hedge. He landed headfirst, with just his black boots sticking out.

"He's fine," called one of the organisers scurrying past. "Just got some thorns in his backside." It has been said that the spirit of Agincourt lives on in team-chasing.

"Hubby riding today, I see, Mrs P." There was an obvious gleam of satisfaction in Kinsman's eye, no doubt caused by

Rupert's unceremonious unseating. "He should be more careful, that sort of accident can prove fatal at his age."

There was something about the way he'd said it, that made my flesh crawl. Over the past few years, Rupert had been 'dropped' on several occasions and it had been one of these incidents that had forced him to give up riding point-to-point completely. Kinsman walked away, but not before I'd glimpsed another smug smile of satisfaction. The old psychic alarms bells weren't just ringing, they were belting out the *Halleluiah Chorus*!

Suffering nothing but a badly bruised shoulder, Rupert was confined to the kitchen for a few days and decided to spend the time cleaning some of the old tack that had been hanging around for years. Pris and Adam arrived with the details of their new business venture – although Adam was less than excited about becoming the proud owner of a three-storey Victorian mill building, with dodgy drains. The asking price had been cheap because it had been leased out in small sections to about thirty local antique dealers, all with cast-iron contracts to boot. There was a run-down 'caff', which Pris intended to turn into an up-market café, where 'ladies who lunch' could go to spend a few hours and also, hopefully, several hundred pounds.

"It's going to be called 'The Witch's Kitchen' and when it's been decorated, and with that old black ranged leaded up, it will be really smart. And instead of putting up the rents, I'm to receive a percentage of all sales."

"But what are you going to do about catering?" From the tone of his voice, it was obviously a question Adam had asked on numerous occasions and, as yet, gleaned no satisfaction from his wife's response. "I mean, you can produce a pretty mean casserole and Sunday roast, but you're not exactly adventurous in *that* department, are you, love? 'Ladies who lunch' aren't going to want your *only* two specialities of the day on a permanent basis."

Pris scowled, partly miffed by this lack of domestic solidarity and partly because the dog was resting its head in her crotch in the hopes of receiving the remains of her sandwich.

"Why not round up some of the local farmer's wives who do

the Farmers' Market, that way you'll be able to offer home-produced ... damn!"

"What is it?" I asked. Rupert had been saddle-soaping a saddle that had belonged to an old favourite of his, and had not used it since the horse had been put down some years before. It was a heavy, old-fashioned saddle and he'd been working soap into the under-side.

"I've cut my finger on something sharp ... wait, it's a piece of card wedged under the tree!" He worried at it with his fingernail and finally extracted a carefully folded piece of paper "What the ...?"

"It's a fetish," said Adam slowly, as Rupert unfolded the paper to reveal a simple esoteric design.

"But what's it doing in *that* saddle?" I asked. "It hasn't been used for years."

A familiar hiss escaped from Pris. "And who had their hands on that saddle last? Bloody Jackie Pratt! Don't you remember, she was always hanging around the yard about the time Weyland had to be shot? The saddle was all muddy and none of us wanted to clean it because it was all too upsetting. She volunteered to take it home with her, and she kept it for weeks."

"Yes," replied Rupert, "and I actually had to go and retrieve it myself."

I suddenly remembered the smug expressed on Kinsman's face and wondered if the fetish-placer had told him about the old charm. What she hadn't known was that the saddle hadn't been used again, and had been kept in the loft above the tack room ever since ... but it was near enough to send out its malevolent impulses to anyone who spent a lot of time in that building. Was this Jackie Pratt's revenge for not being allowed in to our personal and magical lives?

"What are you going to do?" Pris and I asked in unison.

Rupert carried on polishing the leather without answering, but we all knew score. He would bide his time but the malice would be returned to its sender.

With the question of the fetish still in my mind, I was surprised when, some days later, Gordon cornered me in the kitchen garden and asked if he could talk to me about his romance. Escaping to the kitchen garden with a cup of coffee, even in winter, is my idea of a peaceful five minutes but today wasn't going to be my lucky day. Granny, it appeared had been meddling with a vengeance and Gordon was rather alarmed by the things she'd been saying to him. He's a good, reliable lad and a wonderful horseman, and I didn't like to think of him being upset, even if his girlfriend did give cause for concern.

He leaned against the brick wall and ran a finger over the pointing. "She also said that I wouldn't be allowed to stay on in the yard, if I carried on seeing Christine," he said, almost in tears.

I sighed with exasperation. Whilst I appreciated Granny's viewpoint, threatening the lad was not going to produce the desired effect. Her own daughter, Rupert's stepmother, had been so meek and mild that the old girl had probably forgotten that when you tell the younger generation they *can't* do something, it usually makes them all the more determined to thwart you at any cost.

"Granny is concerned," I said slowly. "And as far as the Coven is concerned, she has a right to be, but there is no need for you to worry about your job. We would never ask you to leave because of ... your involvement with this girl."

"But why doesn't anyone like her?" he naively asked.

"It's got very little to do with her as an individual, and everything to do with her family's beliefs. *They* will be the ones who won't let it rest. You shouldn't have told her you were a witch." From what I could gather Christine was as dim as a Toc-H lamp, but I could hardly say so to Gordon's face. Neither did I want to admit that we'd heard the family had their sights set on bringing a stray lamb back to the fold and nailing him firmly to their cross.

Pentecostals, as far as I am concerned, are the most acrimonious, highly poisonous and malignant sect of all. And I should know, since they were a strong feature of Welsh religious life in the early part of the century, and my family came originally from that neck of the woods. The services are enthusiastic and rousing with a strong emphasis on music and participation on the part of the congregation, where 'speaking in tongues' is assumed to be a form of spirit baptism. And they'll damn anyone to hell and perdition for very little reason, even their own — never mind anyone who had admitted to being a witch. Gordon's naivety would be his undoing.

"But what do *you* think I should do?" he asked. After all, I was still Dame and he was still a member of the Coven. "I'm getting flack from all sides."

"I can't answer that, Gordon, but I do think you are much too young to be thinking about settling down with *anyone*, and so I can't see what all the fuss is about. Just don't let anyone put any pressure on you to anything until you're 100% sure about how you feel. Not Granny, your parents, Christine ... or her parents. It's got to be what *you* want but it will mean leaving the Coven were you to make the arrangement a permanent one. There's nothing we can do about that, I afraid."

He pushed away from the wall and shuffled off back to the stables. "I know. Just so long as I don't have to leave the horses," he muttered as he walked away.

I sat back and closed my eyes against the sun. *Rooted and bound, rooted and bound ...,* I thought with a smug smile. Granny might be meddling to end the romance but it was far easier to tie the lad to something by love than through bullying or fear.

The following day Granny turned up at coffee time with a large tray of home-made cakes and buns for Pris to try out at the Witch's Kitchen. We were rather dubious about trying *anything* as they'd been on the back seat of her car, but they did look appetising. She'd been over to a nearby village to visit May Butterworth, whose baking skills in the area were almost legendary. From what I'd heard, there had been some rivalry between the two women in the dim and distant past but I couldn't for the life of me remember what it had been about.

"I didn't think you liked May Butterworth," I said, fishing for information.

"I don't, but she does make exceedingly good cakes," replied the old witch with a cackle.

Later that day, as I was coming out of the newsagent's, I bumped into Gordon's father, who was known to all as 'Young' Joe, on account of him being 'Old' Joe's son. "Do you know what that ol' bugger's up to?" he asked without preamble, and without having to think I'd guessed he was talking about Granny.

"What's she done now?" I replied, not really wanting to know the answer.

"I were coming home the other night, well past midnight it was, and I saw this great black shadow squatting in my garden. Can you guess what she were doing?" I shook my head. "*She were pissing on the path!* All I could see were this great white arse gleaming in the moonlight! Gave me quite a turn, I can tell you." He frowned for a moment and then went on. "Mind you, if it's summat to do with getting rid of that daft lass of his, I'll not mind." And with that he walked off. Loosely translated for the non-initiate, it appeared that Granny *had* started meddling with Gordon's romance with a vengeance.

With the start of spring, life on the farm works it own kind of magic. At Candlemas, we see the first of our lambs, which also heralds the old Imbolc – the start of the old Celtic lambing season. Although our lambs are safe and snug in the lambing sheds, it never ceases to amaze me that these fragile little creatures can withstand the freezing weather conditions that can bring snow and icy winds and driving rain. This is a true marker on the turning of the year.

Spring Equinox

According to most 'witchy' books, the Spring, or Vernal Equinox always falls around 21ˢᵗ March but, owing to the idiosyncrasies of our calendar, the actual date is not constant and can vary anywhere around that time. The Equinox marks the moment when the Sun crosses the celestial equator, moving from south to north. For the next six months it will stay in the northern hemisphere of the sky, before crossing the equator at the Autumnal Equinox and returning to the south.

As we've explained before, this is why the Coven prefers to observe the equinoxes and solstices rather than the traditional Wiccan calendar dates; we work with the actual changing tides of the cosmos rather than some dubious Church calendar dates that now have Celtic names and a tenuous grasp on tradition. Sometimes traditions have to change and precession eventually alters the seasons, but the equinoxes and solstices remain constant and mark the times and tides of the year for us, exactly the same as it did for our early ancestors.

Spring Equinox was the date set for the grand opening of the Witch's Kitchen, and there'd been a great flurry of activity as we all pitched to help with the preparations. I didn't consider it to be an auspicious time to start a new business as, from personal experience, I've always found the tides around the Spring Equinox to be extremely dangerous and unpredictable, as Julius Caesar found to *his* cost. It's often a time for great changes and upheaval, with a knock-on effect that can last right up to the Summer Solstice.

The interior of the café was now crisp and bright, although the rest of us weren't convinced by the collection of stuffed animals peering out at the diners from their glass prisons but ... well, Pris has always had a 'thing' about stuffed animals and it's her business. The collection had started when she decided to visit a similar venture she'd heard about some 70 miles away, and prudently (or so he'd thought) Adam had elected to wait in the car to read his newspaper while she snooped around.

Nearly half an hour had passed and as he turned the pages of the broadsheet, his eye caught sight of a female figure attempting to wrestle a 12-point stag's head through the narrow shop doorway. From where he sat, it looked as if the stag had the advantage. Adam slowly lowered the newspaper and open-mouthed watched as his wife advanced towards the car, presenting a surreal, anthropomorphic image of a stag's head on a woman's body – complete with mini-skirt and four-inch stilettos!

"How the hell are we going to get it in the car, love?" he said wearily.

"Don't be silly, of course it will go in."

"You couldn't get it through the bloody shop door, so how do you expect to get it in a Metro?"

Pris stopped and stared, forgetting they'd borrowed their son's car for the day, but as we've often said before, once Pris gets an idea in her head, there's no stopping her. The long-suffering Adam travelled home lying flat in the back of the car, holding the stag's head in a meaningful embrace and trying to prevent the points of the antlers from impaling his wife whenever she applied the brakes.

We later discovered why the thing had been such a 'bargain'. The skin on the muzzle had shrunk, exposing a rim of white plaster underneath, and giving the impression of an advert for a well-known brand of toothpaste. Added to that, one of the glass eyes had a tendency to roll, which meant the 'ladies who lunch' would fall under the manic gaze of a leering stag – very Horned God indeed, but not over lunch! Another acquisition was a fox with a similar expression. Only this was due to it having been rammed into a much smaller cardboard box, which had not only distorted the mask but had also given it a curly tail like a husky! The company (to date) was completed by an owl minus some tail feathers and a stuffed stoat, for whom time had metamorphosed its ferocious snarl into another manic leer. Adam's response to his wife's interest in a full-sized bull moose was: "Don't even think about it!"

What the new waitress made of her employer's penchant for surrounding herself with dead animals, it was hard to say. She said very little but I had the feeling that she was listening to everything, and missing nothing. We didn't have long to wait.

It was the sort of filthy wet Monday that always took me back to my schooldays, when everywhere smelt of damp gabardine. The Witch's Kitchen was too far from town for any except the real die-hards to brave the weather, and so Rupert and I were summoned over there for a late lunch in order to minimise the waste. We were just sitting down to what looked like being a mammoth trenching session, when Rupert surprisingly asked Abi, the waitress, to join us. Not being the most sociable of folk, especially where strangers were concerned, it was most out of character.

We'd finished off Brenda Macinroy's French onion soup and were about to start on Buffy Lambert's *lamb marinade*, when a party of late lunchers arrived and the lamb was off ... and onto their plates! The local farmers' wives were doing Pris proud and half the success of the place was the fact that she was offering freshly home-cooked food every day. Even the parsimonious antique stall-holders were coming down from their dusty eyries for lunch, even if it was only for a sandwich or a bowl of soup ... and recommendations were bringing in visitors from further a field. Locals knew the cauldron and besom by the old range were for real; the visitors merely thought it quaint. By the time everyone had left, we were finishing off with coffee and Anna Robson's *rhubarb compote* ... and nothing had gone to waste.

"So did you work with a group before moving here?" Rupert suddenly asked Abi without any further preamble.

"I'm not sure what you mean," she answered hesitantly, looking uncertainly from me to Pris, and seeing that both of us were just as surprised by his question.

"I'm sorry," replied my cunning old Man, "I had the impression that you were a witch, albeit a young one."

"I don't know if I am or not," the girl replied nervously. "I did belong to a group in the Midlands, but there was something ... not quite right about it. I couldn't say what exactly, but things just didn't *feel* right and so I left. That's why I'm here, they sent their fetch after me and I couldn't get away from him. They kept trying to draw me back in."

"What form did it take?" asked Rupert, then seeing the girl's hesitation added, "The fetch?"

Abi looked blank. "It was just a member of the group. He was called 'the coven fetch'. Am I missing something?"

Pris snorted. "These people are a bloody menace! What did *he* tell you he was there for?"

"His job was to act as a go-between, take messages and summon people to the coven, to 'fetch' them, I suppose. He was sent to coax me back and kept coming to the flat, banging on the door. In the end I had to move to get away from them."

Before Pris could open her mouth, Rupert began to explain. "A fetch isn't a human being, Abi, it's an astral entity created by a coven or individual to over-look, or carry messages between the different psychic levels. It's like having an astral working sheepdog, because they can run amok if not kept under control. It's something else belonging to traditional Craft that has appeared in books without the authors having the slightest understanding about the magical aspects. The meaning has been taken literally by people with no genuine magical training and applied to what they see as being their version of witchcraft, or Wicca. This is why the Old Ways are being plagiarised and turned into something completely bogus in order for the role-playing to continue. Unfortunately, there is a whole new generation of potential witches who have no access to genuine Craft because they don't know it exists, thanks to that lot."

Abi looked around the table at each of us in turn, and the light slowly dawned. "You lot *are* for real, though, aren't you?"

We said nothing and Rupert looked at his watch as a sign that it was time to go. "How did he know?" whispered Pris in my ear, as we were leaving.

"How did you know?" I asked as we drove home.

Rupert just gave an infuriating chuckle and patted my knee. "Oh, when you've been a witch for as long as I have, you learn to recognise these things," he added, exasperatingly.

Once Abi began to relax in our company, she kept Pris amused for hours relating her experiences with the Midlands coven. It transpired that the couple who ran it were media junkies, who had recently appeared on television and not given a very good account of themselves, not to mention the rubbish they were spouting about paganism *per se*.

Now referred to as the 'Odd Couple', we learned that, although not the most prepossessing of sights, they insisted on working sky-clad on every occasion, with cold water being flicked on the women's breasts to make the nipples stand out. Pris was reduced to tears of laughter at the thought of the male OC prancing around stark naked, banging his drum to the midsummer chant of ...'*The sun has got his hat on, hip-hip-hip hooray ... the sun has got his hat on and he's coming out to play ...*'

On the occasion of an initiation, a newcomer was hauled in to take the part of 'initiatorix', when she'd only been a member for a couple of weeks and had just popped in to deliver a bag of cooking apples! The initiation consisted of the naked couple facing each other with the chap standing on the girl's feet, while the HP and his drum and limp lingam, banged out a chorus of '*Robin Hood, Robin Hood, riding through the glen ...*' from the old television series. By this time Pris was convulsing and had to be given a large slug of *Famous Grouse* before listening to any more.

What was even more insidious than all this clowning around was the fact that Abi is a natural witch (albeit an untrained one), and the Odd Couple hadn't been slow in spotting this. On the pretext of letting her experience *their* power raising, they encouraged her to open up and empower the Circle (under the OC's guidance, of course), while all the time they were drawing off *her* in the worst form of magical exploitation. No wonder they wanted her 'fetched' back! It was this raw, natural energy that Rupert had sensed when he first met her in the Witch's Kitchen.

Having convinced the girl that the Coven wasn't into exploitation, magical or otherwise, Pris and Adam took Abi up to one of our working sites in the woods, having assured her that robes and thermals would more than likely be order of the day. In all the years she'd been a 'practising Wiccan', she had never once worked outside after dark, under the stars, and it all became very tearful. It looked as though we might have discovered a new Coven member.

We've often remarked that potential members are a bit like a number 29 bus: you wait for ages for one and then two come along together. The second manifestation came in the form of the unfortunate woman Rupert had savaged in Castor & Pollux some months earlier, but this time it was Pris who had brought home the trophy, along with some tantalising gossip. She'd called into the shop for a coffee and Gerry was showing her some of the new merchandise that had been delivered that morning.

"Here, it says in this book that a curse can be lifted by a liberal application of white candles, clear quartz crystal and white lily essence," said Gerry, deliberately winding her up.

"Not one of *mine*, it wouldn't," she retorted.

"And what about this?" asked Gerry, handing her a box bearing the banner 'Witches Tool Kit'. On opening it, to reveal a pentagram-shaped display, the first thing Pris saw was the wand – a pencil-thin stick that came in two pieces that screwed together. The *Book of Shadows*, was an equally unimpressive paper leaflet which she couldn't even bear to open and read.

"Why on earth are you stocking this?" she asked.

"We're not," he replied, "but folk keep asking for them and so I thought I'd get one, just so I can put it in the middle of the display with a card saying: *Do you really think this will make you a witch?* A snip at 20 quid, don't you think? What do you think to the Magical Talisman?"

This was a bright blue printed card with a combination of different symbols on it, including £££ signs and the new euro-dollar symbol. "Ah," said Pris, "it's a Euro-witch Kit!"

The next item, which was probably the most impressive in the box, was a wooden altar pentacle – a three inch diameter piece of wood with a pentagram scratched in it, and filled with gold paint. There were two white candles, a little larger than those used for birthday cakes, complete with a gold plastic holder and three incense cones complete with a 'consecrated incense vessel', which turned out to be a foil holder usually containing a tea-light.

By this time Pris was helpless with laughter but there was worse to come. There was a 'consecrated water vessel' and a 'consecrated salt vessel' (two more tea-light holders) and a bag of 'Salt from the Dead Sea'. Nothing else in the kit, however, compared with the final item ... the 'chalice'. This was a small wooden eggcup that looked as though any liquid poured into it would immediately soak into the wood. It was so badly finished that any potential witchlet would be chewing woodchips for a week, if they actually stopped laughing for long enough to be able to use it.

Almost crying with laughter, the banter continued for some minutes before they realise someone was listening to their conversation. "Excuse me," said a small, middle-aged woman, "I didn't mean to eavesdrop, but do you think you could answer some questions for me? I'm becoming very confused."

Her name was Carole, and she has some very interesting information to impart. When they both were firmly ensconced in the alcove (the sofas now replaced by cane chairs) with a fresh coffee each, Pris learned that this was indeed the poor soul who'd attracted Rupert's wrath over the triple goddess some months before.

"I didn't take too much notice of him, because you meet some really strange people in these sort of shops," she said in a low voice, so as not to cause offence. "But afterwards I got to thinking and so much of what he'd said actually made sense. Anyway, last week I went to a pub moot at the Duck & Ferret, which was being run by the manager, who was saying the most outrageous things ..."

Pris's senses were immediately on auto-alert. "Such as?"

"He was telling the group that he could trace his tradition back to the Stone Age. Oh, it gets worse ... or better, according to your perspective," she said, as Pris failed to suppress a laugh. "Apparently, the founders of his tradition came from Atlantis, via a wormhole in the universe ... no, stop it! He *was* serious, but what I found even more frightening, was that most of the people there were taking it all in. Several of us made the excuse of going to the bar for a drink, but we legged it."

"And this chap said he was the *manager* of the pub?"

"Well, relief manager, which is why I thought he should be okay. What I'm really trying to say is that it made me think even harder about what that man said to me in here. To be honest, I'd rather be thought a fool by him, than treated like a gullible idiot by that other one. Is there any way of getting in touch with him?"

"Grandad wants to see you," said Gordon one morning. "He said it was important."

The old man had been ailing for some months and as it was me he'd asked for, I thought I'd better get round to the cottage as quickly as possible, but without showing any unseemly haste. The district nurse was already hovering around but there was a lot of shouting going on and finally she emerged with an expression like a smacked bottom. Obviously Old Joe wasn't one of her favourite patients, and his reputation for shooting crows and magpies from his 'hide' in the outside lavatory would have been common gossip. There was no sign of the shotgun, but he probably kept it under the bed.

"And just see that you take that medicine," she called in an authoritarian tone from the front door.

The old man was propped up against the pillows with a mulish expression on his face. As soon as the door closed with a bang, he leaned over and emptied the glass into a chamber pot he obviously kept there for the purpose. At least, I *hoped* it was discarded medicine, since the colour of the liquid would have given medical science cause for concern!

"You know why I want to see you," he said, and then carried on without any further preamble. "*You* won't beat around the bush and try to convince me I'm not dying. Well, I am and I haven't got long left, so I need you to do a couple of things for me and not let that daughter-in-law get her own way, like she did when the Missus went. The Old 'Un and May Butterworth were here yesterday, not that I'd ever expected to see those two together in the same room, and my bedroom at that, but they agreed that I should talk to you."

"Yes," I said thoughtfully. "They're as thick as thieves at the moment and yet I always thought they loathed each other."

Old Joe chuckled, obviously enjoying some memory. "They fell out over *me*. Had 'em fighting like cats, clawing and kicking and biting. Took four blokes to haul 'em off each other."

It wasn't easy to imagine Granny, or May Butterworth for that matter, rolling around in the dirt and fighting over a man. I looked at Old Joe with new respect.

"What exactly ..."

He reached out and grabbed my hand, showing amazing strength for one so near death's door. But there was also fear. "Gabrielle, I don't want to be buried in no graveyard by some vicar. The Missus ... well, she didn't mind where she went but I do. The vicar can say what he likes over my coffin if it keeps the rest of the family quiet, but I don't want to be buried in no Christian soil. I want you to ask your Man if he'll find me a bit of a plot ..." The brusque voice wavered, afraid of refusal.

"I promise we *will* take care of you," I said gently, holding his hand. "Give Joe a letter stating that you want us to arrange the burial and then there can be no disputing it when you've gone." I didn't like to tell him that the dead have no rights over their own disposal, but I trusted Young Joe to do the right thing by his father.

"And I want one of them willow caskets ... according to the Old Ways. I'll not be any trouble to him when I'm in the ground."

Earth to earth.

It's always more heart-rending when a large, strong man or animal is reduced to a dependency on others. Old Joe had been a part of our landscape and many are the times he'd snuck-up on Rupert coming home from a teenage night out at the local pub, his cat-like tread making no sound despite those great heavy boots. The first Rupert had ever known that the old man was about, was when a large hand descended on his shoulder out of the darkness, which had never failed to scare him out of his inebriated wits. I knew there would be no hesitation on his part in granting the old man his first and final request.

Dust to dust.

None of us could ever remember there ever being any talk of Old Joe actually being a member of the Coven, as he had always occupied one of those shadowy realms that lie between witch and countryman. In the old days these functions would have over-lapped on numerous occasions, and much of what today is referred to as 'witchcraft' was once basic country lore. It might have been Granny who taught us to tell the maze and call the spirits, but it was the old man lying upstairs waiting for death, who had taught us the healing power of herbs and to divine using the behaviour of birds.

Ash to ash.

Roodmas

It's always a bit daunting when witches who have become familiar acquaintances unexpectedly ask you to take part in one of their celebrations. This is especially true when the invitation has come at a time when you have just announced that you are not doing anything on that particular date. Rather than trying to mumble some lame excuses, it's sometimes easier all round just to bite the bullet, and accept with as much good grace as you can muster.

Of course, since the publication of *Coarse Witchcraft: Craft Working*, it's highly unlikely that any members of the Coven would be invited anywhere ever again, in case their hosts find themselves exposed in the next volume!

And so it came to pass that Guy and Gerry were neatly cornered into spending Roodmas in the company of five very queer witches (and *they* used the word advisedly) following the invitation from one of their very good customers. They were told it would be a traditional seasonal gathering, with just a simple ritual.

At the appointed time, our 'boys' arrived, resplendent in their elegant black robes, warm cloaks and bearing gifts of wine and one of Gerry's wonderful cakes, decorated with a spiral pattern picked out in silver balls. "As we hadn't been asked to take part in any formal part of the rite, we were simply looking forward to being able to relax and let someone else take the floor," explained Gerry.

"That was mistake number one. Mistake number two was in taking it for granted that everyone present, knew what they were doing. I mean Gaby dear, *we* might be gay, but this lot were hysterical!

"We were greeted by our customer, clad in see-through silver muslin, a silver leather thong and an inordinate amount of body glitter. On a professional drag-queen this might have been pass-able but on a middle-aged, balding gentleman of more than ample proportions, it bordered on being frightening. Before Guy and I could exchange a glance, his partner, whom we'd only met on a couple of occasions, flew down the stairs and embraced us warmly. He clung onto Guy for a little longer than was necessary, leaving a generous application of Revlon foundation smeared down the front of Guy's immaculate little black number.

"Host Number Two was clad in a short Byronic nightshirt split to the waist to reveal a shapely pair of legs, shown off to perfection in gold mesh leggings. The fetching black French knickers, worn tantalisingly over the top, co-ordinated beautifully with highly pol-ished leather jackboots. I looked away just in time to catch the look of abject horror on Guy's face. Swiftly, to the point of rudeness, and before he went into shock, I pushed him towards the sitting room where a welcome log fire crackled. I began to prattle on about the cold ... anything in fact, to keep my mind off those French knickers, in spite of just having caught a fleeting glimpse of them vanishing back upstairs again."

Apparently Gerry spent the next ten minutes plying Guy with *Grouse* until he'd smoothed his partner's offended sensibilities. Their *sotto voce* conversation was finally interrupted by the arrival of Dick Whittington, sporting an enormous cod-piece and accom-panied by his Cat dressed in fishnet tights and four inch stiletto-heeled boots. In their plain black robes, it appeared that Guy and Gerry were distinctly under-dressed for the occasion.

"There was a sound of footsteps on the floorboards above, and Host Number Two re-appeared with a companion. It seemed that this young lady had gone to bed the minute she arrived (as you do in someone else's house) and Lord Byron had been tucking her in when the 'boys' arrived. They weren't introduced to her as she was painfully shy; a fact that wasn't immediately obvious as she was dressed from head to toe in scarlet and sporting a cleavage that would have rivalled Dolly Parton. Gerry was busy trying to decide whether she was supposed to be a little devil, or a circus clown, as the strategically placed pom-poms made it a difficult decision. Guy wondered through his haze of *Grouse* whether they'd got the dates muddled up and they were all going Trick or Treating instead.

Pris and I decided to call round to the shop for the next instalment. Pris, being highly delighted that someone else was on the receiving end of 'What Witches Do', settled down in a chair with a coffee, ready to gloat. Guy, as handsome as ever, reclined in another chair while Gerry re-opened the batting ...

"Our muslin draped host handed out what looked like large green pencils, which confused us even more ... were we going to be asked to knock up a quick sketch of the proceedings as they happened? A quick explanation followed, with instructions on how to bend these things in half when we were all in place. Bendy fluorescent wands were a new magical invention to us, but when in Rome and all that, and we meekly followed the small procession out into the garden, where a large need-fire was burning.

"It came as a bit of a surprise to be informed at the last minute that we were appointed to work two of the quarters, but girding our loins we prepared to do our bit. I've never witnessed the quarters being manned by a Dick and his Cat before but we'd been assured that all these people were Initiates, so who were we to question? At the centre of our little company sparkled our High Priest, while lurking in the shadows behind him stood Host Number Two, with his arms wrapped protectively around our shy little devil, Dolly. Her shyness must have been crippling.

"With a flourish of muslin that hovered dangerously near to the flames, our High Priest opened the proceedings. The familiar banishing pentagrams were flung in all directions as he left nothing to chance. Nothing untoward was going to get near this ritual; in fact nothing of any description was likely to either. *Surely* the invoking bit was going to come in a minute? As the last bastions of defence were left hovering in the air, the silence was broken by a bellowed instruction to bend!

"We all know that a certain amount of risqué fun happens at a lot of witchcraft gatherings, but it seemed a bit early in the night for any bending, especially in mixed company. Then we realised it was the green wands he was referring to. Dutifully we all waggled the hard plastic about and lo and behold the things burst into light. I was suddenly reminded of a group of giant glow-worms, all hovering at waist height. The Beltaine rite was truly underway."

Guy took over the narrative in his smooth, dark chocolate voice. "The Dick's glow worm wavered in mid air for a second before the guardians of the eastern gateway were summoned. As spontaneous calls go, I had to admit that this was impressive. All and everything that could possibly be attributed to the eastern quarter was mentioned in almost poetic terms. The glow-worm took a nose-dive at one point, but it was soon aloft again and hovering steadily. After a respectful pause it was the turn of the Cat. Another glow worm teetered above head height, and another beautiful call issued forth. Surprisingly, this glow-worm also took a nose dive at one point, but over all the performance was admirable ..."

"Then it was my turn," interrupted Gerry, "and turning outwards I raised my glow-worm and waited. The seconds ticked by and still I waited, sure that any minute now I would feel the old familiar inner stirring, which confirms to me that I have made my contact. I waited a few moments longer, with my throat tightening and absolutely nothing magical stirring whatsoever, the night air remained a blank canvass to me. I heard Guy discreetly clearing his throat (coded language for 'Get a move on, I'm cold/bored/thirsty or need a piddle'). The awful realisation dawned that this gathering was totally and utterly devoid of any magic, the High Priest had seen to that with his flourish of banishing pentagrams.

"It seemed that the Wise Ones were making damned sure that I didn't go along with this charade. Improvising swiftly while making mental apologies to any affronted guardians, I drew what I hoped would pass as a deeply mystical symbol in mid air, and turned to face the centre with a benign smile on my face. A murmur of approval rippled around the Circle and I was relieved to see that everyone seemed duly impressed (including myself!).

"It was just a bit disconcerting to catch a glimpse of a twinkle in Guy's eye as he addressed the quarter. Credit where credit is due, he managed to give a good account of himself, the only trouble was that I happened to recognise just exactly *what* he was addressing. It's not for nothing that he shares that magical catch-phrase with Adam," said Gerry, glancing meaningfully in Pris's direction. "*If in doubt - get the old dark forces out.* Banishing pentagrams or no banishing pentagrams, *something* took great glee in turning up at the party.

"Suddenly the peace of the sacred space was shattered. There was a loud four-lettered expletive from the Cat as she wobbled on a broken flagstone and pitched into a rose bush, laddering her tights as she fell. Undeterred our High Priest launched into a long spiel taken straight from the *Gospel of Aradia.* This was a tad unexpected but by now we were learning to roll with the punches. The Dick had leapt to the Cat's rescue and felt compelled to drag her into the darkened undergrowth to administer some emergency first aid. From the ensuing noises, which were reminiscent of a sink plunger unblocking a drain, I can only imagine that he had insisted on kissing it better."

Guy crossed one slim leg over the other and took up the tale. "Aradia was well into his stride by this time, and a long garbed speech ensued about the meaning of the night's gathering. It didn't seem entirely accurate to me given the gender ratio of the company but by that time I was so cold and angry with Gerry for getting us into this farce that I seized on it as a welcome sign that things were drawing to a close. Sure enough, the moment came to bless the feast, and at this point Dolly, the little red devil got a shock. As you know, when the Horned God is summoned by an imperious Aradia, he does not argue.

"Dolly was unceremoniously thrust away to fend for herself as our hosting Horned God dived to his knees and slid gracefully across the grass, to arriving at the billowing muslin folds of Aradia, encased in that silver thong.   Mutely, Dolly turned her eyes on me but I gave her a glowering look from under my hood and that was warning enough.   In fright she turned towards the Dick and kindly though he might have been feeling, a piercing scowl from the Cat soon put paid to any altruistic tendencies *he* might have been going to have.   Retreating further into the shadows, Dolly had to be content with hugging the dead stump of a tree.

"At last, the rite, such as it was, ground to a halt but not before we'd all been instructed to jump through the flames to ensured continued fertility for the coming year!   This seemed quite incongruous considering that there were two gay couples, the Dick and his Cat and Dolly the Clone in the company!   Host Number Two began with a flourish and at the fire's edge he took off in quite a spectacular leap, with arms and legs flailing, and those French frillies sailing uncomfortably close to the flames.   But it is the sight of middle-aged flab exposed under ruched-up muslin, genitals held snug in a silver posing pouch and skimming through the fire-light, is one I will carry to my grave.

"As we filed indoors, I chanced to pick up some crumpled sheets of paper from the shrubbery.   Written out neatly, in print just large enough to read by the light of a glow worm, were two lovely calls to the guardians of the east and south.   So much for our experienced Initiates, then?   As coven gathering go, this one was certainly different, but I can only hope that this lot are never involved in the re-making of *The Wicker Man*.   I don't think I could stand to see Edward Woodward playing the part in black French knickers and jackboots."

Despite the popular conception of farmers being callous and exploitative when it comes down to livestock and wildlife, no self-respecting countryman will pass a fatally injured animal without stopping to put it out of its misery.   I pulled back the curtains early one morning to find a sickly rabbit sitting in the middle of the lawn. It was suffering from that scientifically-created disease known as myxomatosis and there was only one solution.

"Rupert," I said, "there's a poorly bunny out on the lawn with 'myxy', can you go out and sort it?" A grunt came from under the duvet. I went downstairs to the kitchen to make the tea and each time I looked out, the poor shivering creature was still there. "Rupert," I said, a little more forcefully, banging the tea-tray down on the bedside table.. "Will you *please*, go and deal with that rabbit?"

In exasperation, he flung back the duvet and I followed the noises of him stomping downstairs and out into the boot room. There was the rattle of the gun cabinet keys, the sound of the back door opening and the crunching of footsteps on the gravel. There was a loud bang and the poor rabbit keeled over, its suffering at an end. Then I heard a cheerful voice call out in greeting, "Mornin' Mr P. A grand day for a bit o' shooting." It was the postman, totally unfazed by the sight of a stark naked man, walking around wearing just a pair of wellies and brandishing a shotgun.

But that's the country for you.

Things were a bit more confrontational at the Witch's Kitchen later that day, when 'arfa Kinsman showed up and threatened to test Pris's resolve not to belt him if she got half the chance. Fortunately, it was before the café opened and only Abi and Carole were there to bear witness. Kinsman strolled in and, completely ignoring the two women, who were setting the tables for lunch, made straight for Pris.

She glanced up but his opening gambit caught her by surprise. "Pris, you and I need to get one or two things sorted out. You can't refuse to recognise me as a member of your Tradition because the Old Man himself gave me access to your teachings."

"I can, because you are *not* an Initiate. And you well know the Old Man's not been himself for quite a few years. Whatever he gave you doesn't make you a member of our Tradition."

"Oh, we'll see about that!" he responded, leaning forward across the counter, all pleasantry now evaporated. "If you don't accept me, I can make life very awkward for you, believe me!"

"Is that a threat?" spat Pris, now equally as angry. "Because if it is, you'd better give it your best shot. If you know anything at all about my Tradition then you'll know we don't take kindly to ill-wishing or threats of cursing. And it will be returned to you in ways you've never dreamed possible."

While this exchange was taking place, Carole had positioned herself near the old fireplace and was ready to wield the besom; Abi had fled to the office to get hold of me on the phone. By the time I got there it was all over and Kinsman was nowhere to be seen. Pris, shaken and angry, was nursing a large mug of coffee with its traditional 'rescue remedy' – a large *Grouse.*

"Can you manage on your own for a while?" I asked Abi. "I think Pris could do with some fresh air."

We drove up to the woods and sat on a fallen tree, Pris still clutching the dregs of her coffee and drawing heavily on a cigarette. "By the gods, I wanted to hit him," she said. "I wanted to wipe that smug, smarmy smile off his face right there and then. What do I do, Gaby?"

Some advice is hard to give ... especially when it applies to someone else's Tradition, but as I saw it, there was only one course of action. "You've got to let it go and walk away, Pris," I said. "It's a problem that's only going to get worse, and you know that Kinsman isn't the only one who claims your lineage. The Old Man's been more than a little indiscrete over the past ten years and who knows what else is waiting in the shadows. You're not turning your back on your roots or your ancestors, but you can distance yourself from those who are currently bringing your Tradition into disrepute."

Pris sighed and threw the last of her coffee into the bracken. "Yeah, you're right. I've tried to remain true to my oath but it just isn't possible anymore. You can't remain loyal to something that's no longer loyal to you. Thank the gods, we found the Coven, or we'd really be out on a limb."

"You and Adam took Initiation with us, but it was only really an affirmation of your existing oath. There's very little difference between your ways and ours. We know you have always remained true to your roots, and that's all that matters. It's nothing to do with outsiders ... let them speculate. Besides," I added, "do all these pretenders *really* know what they're getting by taking your Tradition as their own?"

There were some dark, shadowy things that have come out of the Forest of Dean and Pris's Tradition was certainly 'overcast'. There were repercussions in making the Old Ways public property, and I doubted whether any of the folk so desperate for those particular Old Craft roots would be aware of the very *real* dangers lurking in the darkness. The anger and sadness faded from Pris's face, to be replaced by a knowing grin and I knew she was already one step ahead of me. The malediction had been made many, many years before and it had never been, nor could ever be lifted: the Tradition was doomed and the malice and malcontent it bred was manifesting in the political in-fighting between those who would claim it for their own.

"So mote it be!" said Pris getting to her feet and heading back to the car with a much lighter step. She even danced a little jig along the woodland track.

On their heads be it.

It is not until the air is perfumed with the evocative scent of the hawthorn that we actually celebrate 'May' – it's a peculiar musky, female smell that hovers on the breeze and assails the senses. The days had been quite chilly around the beginning of the month and the buds on the may refused to break; then there was the sudden warmth of spring sunshine and the trees were heavy with the sensuous white blossom.

"And after April, when May follows, And the whitethroat builds and all the swallows! Hark, where my blossom'd pear-tree in the hedge Leans to the field and scatters on the clover Blossoms and dewdrops – at the bent spray's edge ..." as Browning would have it.

Summer Solstice

The local Game Fair had grown out of the pagan camp held on our land a couple of year's before. As with most things, the original organisers had moved on, and so the local countryside agencies adopted the idea and developed it into an annual event to showcase rural sports and offer everyone a good day out. It was still held on the weekend nearest to the Solstice and included many of the same people who had played such an active part in that first camp.

Now, three years later, it was a fully-fledged Game Fair, with a centre show-ring, surrounded by craft and country goods stalls, clay-pigeon shooting, lurcher and terrier racing, show jumping and the traditional bonfire with hog-roast. This was more our sort of event, with Richard, Adam and Rupert being the current champions in the team shooting stakes. Not to mention our lurcher being the fastest thing on the block for the second year running. Gerry and Guy had entered their dog but, being a real couch potato, it merely lay down as the others hurtled out of the trap, leaving ours the undisputed champion.

It was a beautifully sunny day as Pris and I strolled round the Fair, the dog sporting his ribbons, proudly attached to his collar. I happened to glance down and saw white foam dribbling from his mouth! Panic set in, until I realised that he was lurcher-height to small children's ice cream cones and that he'd been taking a surreptitious swipe each time he passed. The last lick had removed a whole scoop and he was desperately trying to swallow the evidence before the crime was detected.

The centre show-ring was taken up with the judging of the best-kept children's pony and to our surprise we saw that Rupert had been roped in for the judging. He's not exactly a children-sort of person, and actively loathes Shetland ponies, which he considers to be nasty, evil-tempered little brutes. This event was pure Thelwell, as diminutive tots bustled around the ring, on ponies that were almost as wide as they were high. Rupert's face was giving nothing away, but he wouldn't meet my eye.

A black, leg-at-each-corner, Shetland ambled past and Pris gave a bit of a sniff. "It's not *that* cute!" I said, referring to the child.

"It looks just like Lightning," she replied, with a lump in her throat.

Now Lightning has a tale all to himself, and it's to Pris's credit that she's kept him for nearly 30 years, despite times of great financial hardship, when he's been an awful drain on her resources. We've known about Lightning for years, but he'd continued to live in the valley where Pris grew up and so we'd never actually seen him. In her much younger days, a teenage Pris had been sent to do the weekly shopping, but had hung around the horse sales instead. One lot had been a mare, with her foal being sold separately. The mare had been knocked down to the local knackerman and as she was led away, the foal began screaming and flinging himself about in terror. The knackerman started the bidding, but being a good witch even then, Pris ensured that he had a choking fit, which prevented him from continuing.

The foal was knocked down to Pris but as she explained: "There I was standing in the emptying sale ring, with a hysterical foal, and nothing but a bit of baling band to put round his neck. On top of that, I'd only got my Mother's Morris Minor and I'd spent the housekeeping. [It's nice to know that *some* things don't change!] but I promised him there and then, that I'd never, ever put him back in the sale ring, or part with him."

I knew by now that the old lad must be getting on a bit, but the sight of the little Shetland in the show ring had planted another idea in Pris's head.   Further discussion on the subject was prevented when a young man who was manning one of the stalls, nabbed us. He beamed in a familiar way, and we were just about to head off in the opposite direction when he called us by name.   I frowned for a moment and then realised who he was.

"It Rupert's disciple," I said to Pris.   She looked blank.   "You remember ... the drummer? He and Rupert were joined at the hip during that first pagan camp, and I thought we'd land up having to adopt him. He burned his drum."

"Gotcha."

It transpired that Scot (for that was his name) had taken Rupert's teaching to heart and had gone off to learn more about the countryside before trying to become a witch.   Gone were the long, scraggily locks and beard and we were confronted by a fresh-faced young man in clean chinos and a Tattersall shirt.   He'd got himself a job with a country sports firm – hence his presence at the show – and was hoping to be promoted to manager of a new shop opening up in the area.   He'd already bumped into Rupert, who'd promptly invited him to join us for supper later that day.

"Rupert's getting rather gregarious these days," said Pris, as we moved off.   "Another number 29 bus, do you think?"

Needless to say I made sure that Adam and Pris were also on parade for supper, as Rupert obviously had some hidden agenda in asking a stranger into our home and inviting them to 'take our salt'. It was another illuminating episode in the political intrigues that were constantly dogging our steps these days, despite the fact that we rarely venture far from home, or get involved with the pagan scene at large. Scot had arrived promptly and left at a reasonable hour, leaving the four of us to chew over the information he'd un-wittingly revealed during the meal.

"This is getting too ridiculous for words," said Rupert, "and I deeply resent the inference that the 'pustular postulant' was forced to leave because I couldn't keep my hands to myself!"

"Yes," said Adam gloomily.   "Few men would want to admit to sliding his finger around *her* knicker elastic. The thought is positively frightening."

"The real issue," said Pris pointedly, "is to decide whether this chap is a plant, or not. After all, on his own admission he confessed to having slid more than just a finger under the elastic!"

"Unless he just happened to be in the wrong place at the right time. There was no way that Jackie Pratt could have known he'd met us previously, when he first turned up on her doorstep."

"No, but she didn't waste any time with the name dropping once she' known he'd been to that first pagan camp. Or with the inference that she was more intimately acquainted with us than she was," said Rupert. "Scot was convinced that she had worked with the Coven, and he seemed to know 'arfa Kinsman as well, so I propose we keep him at arm's length until this is all sorted out. It's a pity because it looked as though the boy had put in a lot of effort with the sole purpose of coming back to us in a more knowledgeable frame of mind."

"And it's a shame if she's queered his pitch with us," said Adam, "but I don't want to be looking over my shoulder, wondering who else waiting in the wings."

"I agree," I added. "Since the book came out we've attracted far more attention to ourselves than we could ever have expected. I'm not exactly sure why, considering it was supposed to be a spoof, but I propose we don't take anyone else into the Coven until the interest dies down."

"What about Carole and Abi?" asked Pris. "Adam and I could carry on teaching them without any close Coven involvement, at least until we're absolutely sure of them."

"And Scot's job isn't supposed to happen until next year, so that gives us some breathing space as far as he's concerned. It's a damned nuisance having all this attention," said Rupert, "but I suppose we've brought it on ourselves by going into print, even with such an innocuous title as *Coarse Witchcraft.*"

Rupert had guessed Pris wanted to ask something of him, by the way she kept hanging about and virtually rubbing her shoe up the back of her sock. And because it's the nature of their relationship, he deliberately kept out of her way, just for the sheer delight of winding her up. By tea-time she was nearly in tears of frustration.

"For goodness sake," I said to him, "Can't you see Pris wants to talk to you privately?"

"Of course, I can," he answered with a grin, helping himself to a large slab of fruitcake. "She wants to ask if she can bring that moth-eaten old pony of hers onto the yard, and knows what I think about Shetlands."

"How did you know?" I asked, experiencing another feeling of *deja vue*.

Lightning arrived a week later and it was a sorry home-coming. The poor little chap could hardly put one foot in front of the other because of laminitis, and it took half an hour to get him down the ramp. He was dull-eyed, with sore patches on his skin, and all-in-all had the appearance of a badly-stuffed sofa.

"It might be kinder to have him shot," said Rupert, looking at the pensioner with a horseman's eye.

Pris shook her head firmly, but I knew he was in a worst condition than even she'd remembered. "I've got to give him a chance," she said, leading him into the stable that had been set aside for him. The door closed behind them and I knew a few tears were being shed.

"Isn't there anything you can do?" asked Adam.

"Of course, but there are no guarantees, especially at his age."

In fact, most of the problems had been caused by the wrong sort of care for an aging pony, rather than any deliberate neglect and, compounded by loneliness, he was suffering from a form of depression. The people who had kept him on loan had done their best but a lack of real experience had allowed a lot of problems to develop in the old boy.

Although Pris knew Rupert disapproved of keeping Lightning alive, there were several occasions when she's caught him in the stable administering pig oil and sulphur to help clear up the pony's skin complain, and she often found fresh chopped herbs that she couldn't identify had been added to the feed. By the time, we'd got around to writing this part of the book, the little chap has been given a new lease of life, a different diet and was running around with the other horses, despite his advancing years. Pris had kept her vow and the old pony was home to stay; she had kept to her promise.

Granny's actions were also giving us cause for concern because, to put no finer point on it, she was on the warpath. In all fairness, I think between the Pentecostals trying to poach Gordon and 'arfa Kinsman threatening Pris, she could see the Coven fragmenting and falling apart. Perhaps she thought none of us were doing enough to combat these disruptive elements but we all have our own way of doing things. For some unfathomable reason, Granny and May Butterworth were now inseparable and Granny's marketing efforts on her new friend's behalf might have got her nominated for the Chamber of Commerce 'Businesswoman of the Year' if her motives weren't so downright suspect!

Not only was May Butterworth now making cakes and pies for the Witch's Kitchen, she was also regularly supplying the pub where 'arfa Kinsman was acting as relief manager. It also meant that the scurrilous old bat was busy behind the scenes at the pub, as well as in close attendance when May made her deliveries to the private households in the village. One look at Granny's greasy mits would have been enough to put any self-respecting trencherman off food for life but luckily for May, the Health & Safety people weren't around to slap a Government Health Warning on her bosom pal!

None of us had a clue what the old girl was up to and, even when asked directly if it concerned Gordon, she stared back with those bright blue eyes and refused to answer. If she'd bothered to find out how things were going at the yard, she would have learned that Gordon had jumped at the chance to go up to a small National Hunt yard for a few weeks, when their head lad went on holiday. A few months earlier he would have been reluctant to leave his 'true love' even for a day. *Rooted and bound, rooted and bound ...*

Six of us made the long trek across the fields to the remotest of our working sites. It was Midsummer Eve and as we negotiated the final part of the journey, we stopped to watch the sun disappear behind a distant hill. Summer is actually the worst time to look at the stars, because it is never truly dark; the sun is never more than 15 degrees below the horizon and its glow brightens the sky, even at midnight. In fact, full summer is only said to have begun when the star, Spica, appears in the south west.

Tonight, however, the sky was stained a glorious red-gold, with only a few flecks of cloud floating aimlessly past. We waited with anticipation as we realised that something spectacular was about to happen. Refraction had created a vertical spectrum of colour that seemed to be sinking below the horizon with the sun in the direction of the sea. Because the blue tints were scattered by the air and fragmented, we caught just a fleeting glimpse of that rare green brilliance, known to occultists as the 'green ray', before it disappeared completely. In the deepening twilight, the evening star twinkled towards the West.

This added to the sanctity of the evening's working and each one of us continued walking in silence ... until we came to the clearing. The silence continued, but it was due to dumb-struck horror not reverence. Our magical working site had been defiled in the worst possible way. There were used condoms, empty beer cans and traces of burned foil littered about. The centre of the clearing was scorched from where a large fire had been lit, and the ancient split beech tree had offered a convenient chimney for an impromptu barbeque, the inside of the trunk was now charred and blackened.

Pris bent to pick up a crushed beer can.

"Leave it!" said Rupert angrily. "I'll come back tomorrow and clear it up."

Everyone stood around miserably for a few moments, and then we trudged back the way we had come, but this time in anger and not in any mood for celebration. Not only had our own personal sacred space been defiled, but our land had also been desecrated by morons not fit to be in close proximity to nature. And the powers that be at Westminster want to open the countryside up for all and sundry to rampage across.

It would take Rupert more than just an hour's work in clearing up the rubbish, he would have to spend a considerable amount of time in the magical cleansing – and that would not happen over night. In fact my worst fears were confirmed a couple of nights later when I took a phone call from Pris only moments after putting the receiver down on a call from Gerry. They were both asking the same question ... what did Rupert want with their partners?

"Boy's stuff," I answered.

It would be a long time before we could use the site again for magical working but I hated to think what would be conjured up and left there as a Guardian. Woe betide anyone who ventured there again with vandalism in their hearts! As Pris had commented, even she would think twice about venturing up there if the combined energies of Guy, Adam and Rupert had put the protective boundaries in place!

Lammas

It was Lammastide when we received word that Old Joe had died. The old man had done as I'd asked and left written instructions about his funeral, so it was only a question of deciding who would do what, between us and the family. In the end it was agreed that Young Joe would take care of the arrangements up to the coffin leaving the church, and we would take over from there. There were a few protests from Gordon's mother, who thought the willow casket no substitute for the undertaker's best, but for once she was over-ruled by both husband and son. That she objected to our involvement went without saying.

Nevertheless, he was one of our own, even though he'd not been an active member of the Coven in our memory: and promises had been made. As kids we'd learned our woodcraft from him and as gruff and unbending as he was, there was a kindness concealed beneath the rough exterior. His family had put the funeral arrangements into the hands of Diggit & Bend, a local funeral parlour, so Pris and I slipped in to discuss the plans and to make sure there was no hitch when we took over after the church service.

We also discovered that Old Joe's daughter-in-law was spending more attention to the old man in death than she'd ever done in life. The black hearse, three black limos and masses of flowers. The only fly in the embalming fluid was the willow casket.

Gordon had insisted that his grandfather's wishes had been carried out and compromised by allowing his mother to buy him a smart new suit for the occasion. The undertaker had received explicit instructions that the casket was to covered by a heavily embroidered throw so that the perceived parsimony of the family would not excite comment from the neighbours.

All the mourners were seated by the time we made our entrance and I must confess we created quite a stir: four black riders, in polished boots, pristine breeches, and hunting-black jackets, with riding caps carried on the arm. Rupert, Adam, Pris and myself stood in a row at the back of the church, waiting to escort Old Joe on his last journey. Adam was looking particularly nervous. He doesn't mind the odd slow hack across country but he wasn't that confident in the saddle. He was fidgeting about, then suddenly he was missing and we assumed he was fighting a losing battle with his bladder, or gone outside for a cigarette to calm his nerves.

A couple of minutes later his place was taken by Gordon, who had decided to defy his mother and take his place as the fourth rider. And judging by the speed with which Adam had disappeared, there wasn't going to be any argument or discussion. Gordon looked particularly handsome in his riding kit, but a middle-aged couple and their daughter, who were sitting just in front of us, didn't appreciate his fine appearance. I would have thought Christine would have been proud of her good-looking young man, but somehow Gordon's gesture seemed to have thwarted their sense of propriety. I don't know if it was at that precise moment the girl's parents sensed they were losing the battle for Gordon's soul, but they certainly raised the stakes after that day.

As the pall-bearers lifted the casket, which up until then had been covered by an embroidered purple throw, Old Joe's family led the stampede for the waiting limos. Obviously they were not going to accompany the old man during the final stage of his funeral. The four of us left the church and mounted the horses that had been held at the ready by a groom. We'd managed to borrow an old-fashioned hay-cart, complete with a grey Shire mare, to carry the casket to its resting place on the ridge overlooking the river. The cart was draped in black and Adam was already on board, holding Old Joe's broken shotgun that was to be placed on top of the casket and buried with him. I don't suppose they'll worry too much about a gun license renewal in the Afterlife.

Young Joe and Granny were helped up onto the cart and once they were seated, we were ready to move off. The slow rumble of the wheels on the road, the creaking of the old wooden frame, and the steady tread of five sets of horses' iron-shod hooves set a sombre tone for the hot summer morning. At a slow, walking pace the horses and riders marked the four points: Rupert and I in front, with Pris and Gordon riding behind.

There were more people lining the route of the cortege as it made its way towards the fields and instead of breaking up as the cart rumbled passed, they fell in behind and slowly followed on foot. By the time we turned into the hay field to make our way to the ridge where Old Joe was to be buried, there were over a hundred people walking in silence. When Young Joe turned and saw how many had turned out to pay their respects to his father, he was unable to hold back the tears.

Rupert's men had dug the grave during the previous day and there were six burly farm workers ready to lift the coffin from the cart. They'd all in their time been sworn at, cuffed and bullied by the old man but like the rest of us, most of them had learned their skills under his tutelage. The lid of the willow coffin, with its symbolically broken shotgun, was woven with springs of rosemary and as it was lowered into the ground, the mourners clustered around to throw hand-picked cottage flowers on top.

Rupert and I consigned Old Joe's body to the grave and our eulogy was a highly personal one since he was not only an important part of our lives, he was also one of the last true links with old country Craft. Rupert had sat up most of the night, working to get the words right and when he delivered them over the open grave, there was hardly a dry eye on that hillside. The local kennel huntsman blew 'Gone Away', and as the long, haunting sound echoed across the land, the mounted hunt staff and hounds came passed to pay their last respects.

As the mourners slowly filed away, the farm lads began filling in the grave and only when the last spade-full of earth had been thrown did Young Joe and Granny take their leave. Gordon handed the reins of his mount back to Adam and walked with them down the hill: three of them united in grief and their differences forgotten. We learned later that when they reached the last gate, they'd stopped and looked back. There on the ridge, the sight of the four riders, silhouetted against the clear blue sky of the summer skyline made Granny burst into tears.

If Beltaine is generally the time for rampant sexual urges, those of Lammastide were obviously taking their toll on Gordon. In the weeks following his grandfather's funeral he began looking tired and drawn, and by the end of the month he was looking down-right ill. Finally, Rupert found the boy sitting on a bale of straw with his head in his hands, and felt obliged to ask what the problem was, which was just as well really, since we were entering into the realm of the Horned God.

"Nothing. I'm alright, really I am."

"It looks like it," replied Rupert bluntly. "There's obviously something wrong with you."

The boy answered wearily. "Just after granddad's funeral, Christine ... well, she suggested I stayed over because her parents were away. And ... well, you can guess what happened."

"You've not got her pregnant?"

Gordon shook his head. "I'm not that daft."

"Well, what the devil *is* the matter with you?" said Rupert in his best demanding manner that few can ignore. "Are they trying to force you to join their infernal religion?"

Gordon sighed and surrendered. "They want me to, of course, but the problem is Christine. She wants me to do it every night, and not just once. I'm not getting any sleep and it doesn't matter where we are ... it's out in the fields mostly, now that her parents are back. She won't leave me alone and I don't know what to do."

"Pray for the weather to change," answered Rupert dryly.

Gordon responded with the first smile he'd shown for weeks.

"Are all women like that?"

"No, thank god," said my unsympathetic spouse.

Lammas had always been a strange time of the year. It was the old festival of the wheat harvest and its name came from the Old English *hlafmaesse,* from *hlaf,* loaf and *maesse,* mass = 'loaf-mass'. It was also one of the old quarter-days and the name derives from the custom of each worshipper presenting in the church a loaf made of the new wheat, as an offering of the 'first-fruits'. Although this observance had been incorporated into the church calendar as early as the 8th century, there is evidence for it being much older.

In truth, Lammas celebrations have always been subdued affairs in comparison with the other festivals but for the early farmers, the harvesting of the 'first-fruits' would have been an early indication of feast or famine for the community. These offerings would no doubt have been accompanied by a collective sigh of relief that there *was* a good harvest to come. Despite the fact that Lammastide represents the busiest period in the agricultural year, there is still the element of sacrifice lying just beneath the surface.

In some circles there is the belief that King William Rufus was killed on 2nd August while out hunting in the New Forest in 1100, as part of a pagan sacrifice. There are a number of accounts of his death, including that of the historian William of Malmesbury, who recorded that the king's blood dripped to the earth during the whole journey, in keeping with the old tradition that the blood of the 'divine victim' must be spilt on the ground to ensure the continuing fertility of the land.

True or not, the story symbolises the deep spiritual bond the people have with the land and the deep-seated belief that if the first-fruits are poor, then some form of propitiation must be made now, rather than being left until it's too late. In some parts of the country, Lammas marked the end of hay-harvest, and if this was poor, then there would be insufficient fodder for over-wintering the animals. These harvest customs have survived unchanged for centuries and mirror the sense of belonging and responsibility that is needed in this gruelling partnership.

Several years ago, we lost our entire wheat crop due to bad weather. The incessant rain turned the golden ears to a horrible black mildew and all we could do was to cut it and fire the stubble. I don't know why, but Lammas always represents feminine energies for me and I decided that under the next full moon, I would walk the boundaries of the farm as a propitiatory gesture.

I'd just stepped out of the back door when a shape detached itself from the shadows at my side, making me almost jump out of my skin.

"Nervous tonight, aren't we?" said a familiar voice.

"Pris! What the hell are you doing here?" I whispered.

"If you think for one moment that I'm going to let you go gallivanting off into the night dressed only in a thin, woollen cloak, you've got another think coming." Pris is nothing if not loyal.

"Look, this is my penance, not yours. You don't have to come," I argued in a loud whisper.

"If you don't shut up, I'll bang on the door and let Rupert know what you're doing. And you don't want *that*, do you?"

I didn't, as he would only pour scorn on the whole operation. So in the end I agreed to allow her to accompany me, but the thought of Pris, stark naked under her cloak, save for her hip flask of *Famous Grouse* in her garter, is a memory I shall never forget. We slithered and slipped, tripped and tottered around the boundary as the contents of the hip flask diminished in order to keep the cold at bay. I don't know if the Old Ones were influenced by our gesture but I bet it took them until All Hallows to stop laughing!

"Her parents are hoping the lad gets Christine pregnant, and then he'll *have* to marry her," beamed May Butterworth as Pris encouraged her to enjoy a good gossip. "At the old man's funeral they could see where his loyalties lay and they weren't with 'er."

"But why all this determination to net Gordon?" asked Pris. "He's a smashing chap and a first-rate head lad but that's all he's ever going to be. Financially he's not a good catch."

May Butterworth's cackle was too reminiscent of Granny's to be comfortable. "He's a lost soul and the preacher-man wants to save 'im, even at the expense of his daughter's virtue. Not that the girl could have done anything about it."

"What do you mean?"

"Well, Granny Jay saw to that. I told her that the girl has a regularly order, twice a week, for my vanilla slices and so she used to come over a slip a bit o' summat into the filling." Pris eyed the vanilla slices on the stand with some misgiving. "Oh, those are alright, it was only the ones I saved for Christine that she tampered with. Don't know what she put in 'em but I could do with some of it m'self." The old girl cackled again and leaned forward in a conspiratorial manner. "Young Gordon's been working away for Mr Percy, ain't he? Well, the girl ain't been staying home knitting, I can tell you. She's got a taste for it, and most of the youths in the village have had a generous helping of it by now, I should guess."

What was it Granny had said about May Butterworth making 'exceedingly good cakes'!

Without further ado, Rupert despatched Gordon to another yard in the north of England on the pretext that the owner needed someone to yard-sit while he was in hospital, in the hopes that Christine's behaviour would become public knowledge. This is what we mean about looking after our own, even though none of us approved of Granny's methods. At least we now knew what she was up to as far as the Pentecostals were concerned but it still didn't answer the question of what the old girl was doing at the pub!

Autumn Equinox

It was late afternoon when Adam phoned to ask if we'd seen or heard from Pris. She'd gone out for a ride earlier that day and hadn't returned. By the time we'd all met up in the stable yard to set off to look for her, a very bedraggled horse and rider came in by the field gate. Pris is a highly competent horsewoman but we could all see she'd been badly frightened. The words tumbled out but her relief to be back in one piece was all too obvious.

"I didn't realise how late it was, so I decided to come back along that double hedge at the top of the hay field but within about twenty yards from the end, the horse suddenly shied violently and began rearing. There was nothing at all that I could see to have startled him but it took me all my time to keep my seat and settle him down. Then he began to shake violently and to back up in an attempt to spin round and make off in the direction we'd come from. After a considerable battle, I had him standing still and tried to urge him forward but he just refused point blank to walk on.

"As a last resort, I dismounted, dragged my jacket off and threw it over his head, leading him back, away from whatever it was that frightened him. I took the jacket off and remounted but at this point he plunged up the bank and through the hedge into the field. It took me all my time to hold on. What on earth made him behave like that, I just don't know ... but it was pretty scary ..."

"You can't take a horse down the Hag Track," said Rupert un-sympathetically. "*Everyone* round here knows that. Even the hunt gives it a wide berth because the horses refuse to go along there no matter how fast the chase. Hounds don't like it either, that's why old Charlie makes for that part of the county if they've picked up his scent. The foxes have lived up there undisturbed for as long as I can remember. I thought you knew."

"I *didn't* know," said Pris crisply.

"Well, you do now," answered Rupert with a grin but before he could move out of the way, a piece of well-aimed horse dung took the cap clean off his head.

Bending to pick up another piece, Pris caught one in the bustle. Adam looked at me, and I looked at Adam, and we silently agreed to go back to the house and leave them to it. Pris was obviously over her fright and the muck-fight would end over coffee laced with *Grouse*. Adam and I are used to this kind of behaviour from our respective spouses. At one dinner party, Rupert produced a marga-rine tub full of Bart Simpson water pistols and before the aston-ished guests, he and Pris engaged in a water fight ... reverting to childhood is an excellent way of relieving tension!

The 'track' that Pris tried to ride down is, in fact, an early earthen boundary marker thrown up to separate land owned by different families and believed to date from pre-Christian times. This method created a track wide enough to allow a cart to pass, with high earthen banks on either side, which could run for miles or just a few hundred yards before suddenly coming to an abrupt end. Over the years, these parallel mounds create a 'double hedge', which can be very magical places if they have been left un-disturbed. Our 'hag track' is almost a continuous tunnel of haw-thorn dotted with oak and ash trees, with gaps here and there where livestock have pushed their way through. It no longer marks any boundaries, simply because Rupert's family own the land on either side and have done so for many generations.

Primitive man believed that there was a 'life spirit' that resides within all animate and inanimate things, and happenings such as Pris's encounter are a constant reminder that we do *not* control these natural forces. And it was this 'force' that Rupert and the others had empowered at our sacred site. The weather was still fine and the evenings warm enough to tempt people into staying out of doors, which meant it wasn't long before we heard of the strange goings-on that had affected a group of local teenagers. Fortunately for us, St Thomas on the Poke remains an unspoiled market town, and the inhabitants usually know what's happening on in their midst.

It was Gerry who first alerted us to the possibility of identifying the culprits whose profanity was responsible for our ruined Midsummer rite. If this were the case, then we also knew that they had returned to the woodland clearing again, *after* Rupert had been back to cleanse and magically charge the clearing. Over a beer in the Fox & Hounds, one of the local mothers had asked for Gerry's help and advice when her teenage daughter had suddenly started to have terrifying nightmares.

Gerry asked all the right questions before offering any constructive advice and it was only a day later that the mother came back into the shop with the pertinent information. Apparently her daughter and a group of friends had gone out for another all-night party in the woods, but when they arrived at the place where they'd met previously, they all had the feeling they were being watched. With typical teenage bravado, the group handed out the beer but half-way through the evening something had spooked them so badly that they panicked and fled.

At first they put it all down to a drug-induced reaction but when the nightmares continued some felt the need to talk about their experience. It was soon apparent that none of those affected could give an exact description of what it was that had terrified them, and the impressions were slightly different for each of them. For weeks afterwards they were still being plagued by the fear of being followed, and some were even requiring counselling to help them overcome the fear of being stalked.

Gerry, of course, knew exactly *what* it was that the teenagers had encountered, but he'd been one of the Coven who had seen the defilement of the sacred site, and was less than sympathetic, although he wasn't about to express this sentiment to the worried mother.

A witch of our acquaintance also had a similar experience in recent months, when his own personal site was desecrated by vandals. He pushed on through the undergrowth and eventually came to a previously unknown clearing and in the centre sat a large brown hare. Despite this auspicious sign, there was an overwhelming sense of foreboding and he retreated. Some days later, however, he decided to return with offerings and as soon as he'd made his obsecration, the 'guardian' removed the barriers and he was bade welcome. This type of manifestation is characteristic of 'guardians' and many other kinds of nature elementals and the Adept must learn to recognise, identify and treat them accordingly.

As far as we were all concerned, the crass behaviour of these teenage litter-louts warranted these extreme measures. The land is privately owned and they were in law, trespassers; the litter they'd left behind could have been harmful to all manner of wild-life. Incongruously, the girl whose mother had enlisted Gerry's help, claims to be a 'pagan', as do several of her friends who were there in the woods that night.

This incident perhaps goes a long way to illustrate why we distance ourselves from the so-called 'pagan' scene ... simply because we are not speaking the same language. Or following the same beliefs. Once Gerry knew who the girls were, he recognised them as regular customers in the shop, who were always twittering on about Nature, the goddess and being vegetarian. They bought the books and cultivated the talk but they could still go to a pristine woodland site and leave rubbish behind that could inflict a slow, painful death on any poor creature who, for example, happened to get caught up in one of those plastic beer-can holders!

Here we return to the Old Craft concept of protecting our own, because we cannot - and will not - take responsibility for those who come onto our patch uninvited and desecrate a traditional magical working site. On the other hand, we do know of another magical group who work in the area because we often come across a site that has been recently (although discreetly) disturbed and the obvious signs are there for those with the eye to see. We do not know who they are but we have no objection to them using our woods for their observances because they obviously respect the land. They do not use our personal site for the very same reason. Perhaps they come from a nearby town and do not have any other access to woodland; perhaps they belong to a different Tradition to ours. It doesn't matter, simply because they show themselves to be true witches who do not come to wreak havoc but to pay homage to their gods in time-honoured fashion.

Feigning innocence as to the real cause of the girls' nightmares, Gerry suggested to a couple of them that perhaps they should perform some act of atonement and help clean out a culvert that had become blocked with rubbish during recent heavy rains. After a lot of suppressed sniggering and face-pulling, he was eventually told 'not to talk so bloody silly, that's got nothing to do with *real* magic' and they flounced out of the shop.

All we will say in response, is that the 'guardian' remains in place in our neck of the woods and if any venture there with vandalism in their hearts ... well, as Pris said earlier "So mote it be!"

The year had nearly come full circle and it wasn't long before we discovered what Granny had been up to in her dealings with 'arfa Kinsman. We often find that long-term magical situations or problems resolve themselves between the Autumnal Equinox and All Hallows in a general tidying-up before the end of the year. And prior to the forthcoming Equinox there seemed to be an awful lot of tidying-up that needed to be done.

The two main issues — Gordon and 'arfa Kinsman — were still unresolved and while there had been some significant developments on both fronts, they still remained a problem for the Coven and its members. Christine's behaviour was now public knowledge and 'Young' Joe had wasted no time in informing his son that he was being made a fool of in the eyes of his mates — most of whom had already enjoyed Christine's favours.

Gordon, to his naïve credit, still wanted to believe the best about he girl who'd set his heart aflame and appeared deaf to his father's revelations. That said, he made no move to ask for Rupert's help in ending his three-month stint working away from home. In fact, he made it quite plain that he was more than happy to be a long way from the machinations of Pentecostal pressuring and was more than happy to stay on for a while.

'arfa Kinsman, however, had been around long enough now for everyone in the Coven to be heartily sick and tired of him. His presence in the area was like a winter malady, inasmuch as his malevolence was quiet and non-specific, but the effects were proving to be — if not deadly — certainly unwelcome and unpleasant, and possibly long lasting.

When Rupert discovered that Granny had been tampering with May Butterworth's cakes he was, in the well-publicised style of the Prince of Wales, 'incandescent with rage' and the rest of us made sure we were conspicuous by our absence when he delivered his edict. Not only was Granny's method illegal, she had gone against a specific directive of the Man in Black and that was tantamount to heresy in our eyes. That meant she was formally banished from the Coven and the rest of us were forbidden to intercede on her behalf.

Granny, of course, is *old* Old Craft and a law unto herself. She had set in motion a sequence of cause and effect that was almost impossible to reel back in, even if she'd felt so inclined ... which we were pretty certain she wasn't! The rest of the story filtered through to us via various different channels, the first being Pris, who volunteered to call at the cottage one evening just to make sure the old girl wasn't suicidal or, worse still, homicidal.

She found Granny sitting with her feet nicely tucked up against the old Rayburn, and holding her customary mug of strong tea. Pris pulled up a chair and a mug and they sat in companionable silence for while ... then began to chuckle over a series of gruesome endings for 'arfa Kinsman. Much as it was tempting to go for something permanent, Granny reflected aloud, he wasn't actually worth *that* much effort. The fact that he had to go was without doubt, although the fact that he should be allowed to live she considered to be an inconvenient by-product of Rupert's *edictum*.

The old clock laboured heavily on towards midnight, and the shadows deepened, but still they pondered on the problem. "What about a plague of boils of biblical proportion?" suggested Pris, her thoughts running over Kinsman's attachment to the pustular postulant, and reflecting her own loathing of the pair.

The clock's discordant chimes rang out in the gloom, but it was closer to two o' clock before a satisfied grin suddenly lit up Granny's lined face. With a satisfied grunt, and some grumbling about old bones, Granny unceremoniously showed Pris the door and shuffled off to bed, no doubt to sleep soundly.

According to her custom, the following morning saw Granny up and about as early as ever. A lifetime of late nights and midnight cogitations has conditioned her body to grab whatever sleep it can, yet she is still awake early enough to be abroad before anyone else. A cup of tea, strong enough to double as paint stripper always does the trick, and after two steaming half pint mugs of the stuff, Granny was, as usual, ready to face the day.

Gossip told us that her first port of call was at a small holding some quarter of a mile away, which still went by the quaint local name of Farmer's Bottom. When the new owners moved in two years previously, Granny had made a point of calling and introducing herself. Regular (though uninvited) visits had succeeded in Granny fooling the new folk into accepting her as a well meaning but slightly dotty local character. If the truth be told, Granny, as usual, had her own agenda.

This five, unfarmable acres adjoined Rupert's land, and as an infrequently used right of way ran across a corner of the bottom field, Granny wanted to keep both eyes and ears open for any talk of future building plans. The new people were 'townies' as she disparagingly described them — and pleasant though they may be, they would never be accepted and fully trusted by the present generation of locals. A modest Lottery win and a flashy 4x4 did not compensate for having the 'land in the blood', was the general consensus of opinion.

The one thing that had Granny really rattled was the fact that the couple were raising their two children as vegetarians. It wasn't so much the fact that they chose not to eat meat, as the fact that this enforced diet did not appear to be doing either of the children a lot of good. Pale faced and whining, the two boys were rarely seen playing outside, and when they did, they appeared reluctant to engage in any of the 'normal' games that country children play. The joys of slinging cow pats, chasing hens, climbing trees and falling out of a rope swing were unknown to them — and Granny often muttered to Priss that "it wasn't normal for kids to be so clean." Privately most folk felt that it wasn't normal to be quite so *unclean* as Granny — but these opinions were firmly left unsaid. Dropping a small pot of un-labelled salve into her copious pocket (according to the postman), the old witch had set off to with a firm tread in the hope of catching her neighbours having breakfast. There would be no chance of a decent bacon sandwich — but Mrs Norman did make rather good homemade jam — and a few rounds of hot toast would save Granny the chore of having washing-up to do later.

It transpired that the previous day, Mrs Norton had seen fit to mention that the children were suffering from a very unpleasant form of eczema, which seemed impervious to anything the local doctor had prescribed. Granny's skill with herbs was known far and wide, and today's visit was geared round taking something to cure the affliction. No doubt Granny chuckled to herself as she walked — the Old Gods had never failed her yet when it came to solutions — and her 'mission of mercy' was a convenient beginning to solving the problem of 'arfa Kinsman once and for all. We should have known better than to believe her reluctant promises!

At the Farmer's Bottom, Granny peered closely at the children's heads and faces: it was a nasty case of scald-head and no doubt about it. The cracked skin on the ears, lips and even their eyelids, was weeping and red, and the accompanied itching had the two boys whining even more than usual. Granny having whispered something to them, they both nodded, round eyed and silent, making no protest as she swirled a crooked finger round the pot, before anointing every trace of redness. In less than a minute the boys were running around looking much more cheerful — yelling that they 'didn't tickle' any more.

As she later told a neighbour, Mrs Norman was, of course, genuinely grateful and, insisting Granny stay for toast and a cup of tea, offered to buy the salve. This had, however, vanished back into the darker regions of the waxed coat pocket. "Oh, now I can't go letting you 'av that one, m' dear," smiled Granny, camping up the local accent, "but I'll surely drop you another pot in tomorrow."

Mrs Norton was bemused. "But it's such a trail up the long field — surely I could buy the ointment and save you the trouble of another walk?" she queried.

But Granny wasn't to be persuaded, she simply smiled and said "Oh no, you see this one is promised," and with that she took her leave.

By the time Granny had walked down into the village, the front door of the Duck & Ferret stood wide open, and May Butterworth was just arriving in her old van stacked to the gunnels with trays of homemade pastries. The one-time rivals nodded and exchanged the traditional village greeting which sounded something akin to *"Nah'all"*. No one could remember just what it had originally meant, but roughly translated it was something close to "How are you?" — but as Granny always said — intention is everything.

"What brings you down here?" May had asked, eyeing her with some suspicion.

"Oh, just thought I'd give you a bit of a hand," smiled Granny, as she sallied forth into the dark interior of the pub, carrying a tray of pasties.

The autumn sun not having reached the front windows, the interior was still cold and dark, and Granny had to squint to see that the figure behind the bar was indeed 'arfa Kinsman. He appeared to be checking an invoice, and only looked up when she suddenly manifested in front of him out of the gloom. Before he had time to escape, this terrifying old woman was peering closely at his face, and exclaiming "What's that!"

In the narrow confines of the bar 'arfa Kinsman had little chance of retreating further than a foot, and in some alarm he put his hands to his face. "What's what?" he squeaked, before clearing his throat and attempting to assume a degree of dignity.

Granny shook her head slowly, sucking on her few remaining teeth in true Crone-mode, and with a worried frown, replied: "Oooh, you want to be careful about *that,* lad. There's a lot of it going about at this time of year. Why only today I seen two children fairly afflicted with it." According to the ever-observant May, you could have cut the 'local dialect' with a knife!

By now Kinsman *was* worried, and would have whirled round to look in the large mirrored wall behind him, except that when he attempted to — he found his tie caught in Granny's unwholesome grasp. Before he could react, she'd fumbled in her pocket and produced the pot of ointment. With one finger she flipped open the jar and without further ado, daubed a hefty dollop of goo onto his ear, followed by a liberal application all over his face and neck.

"There," she said, relinquishing her hold on his tie and breaking into a menacingly pleasant smile. "That will sort you once and for all, my lad ... oh aye, sort you good that will.. . never fails to sort doesn't this stuff." And with that, she snapped the lid closed, jammed the jar in her pocket, and left without looking back.

May Butterworth wasn't privy to Granny's 'cunning little plan' but she knew that something had passed between the manager and the old witch, so she hung about to watch developments. 'arfa Kinsman felt at his face, it didn't feel sore, and whatever weird substance the old woman had daubed on him had already soaked into his skin. Examining his reflection, he couldn't see anything wrong, and shaking his head he smirked to himself, obviously thinking that she was as nutty as a fruit cake and probably hadn't a magical bone in her body. The arrival of May's pastries was far more important, and Granny was soon forgotten as he busied himself in the kitchen.

Gossiping with one of the barmaids, May Butterworth discovered that the next morning Kinsman had woken up, full of the joys of self importance, and eager to make a good impression. A large party had booked in for lunch, and he was keen to start chivvying the kitchen staff into an important sounding bustle of activity. The party was made up of Licensed Vitctualler's, and if he could give a good demonstration of his managerial skills, there may even be a chance of a permanent place at the Duck & Ferret.

A lot hinged on the success of the luncheon and, fastening the cuffs on his best blue shirt, he whistled as he took the stairs two at a time. He could shave and finish his toilet later — but first he wanted to make certain that the kitchen *was* a hive of activity. He burst through the swing-doors and was nearly blown back out again by the heat from the ovens, but he was gratified to see the preparations were well under way. Bottles of wine stood ready, gleaming cutlery was waiting on steel trays, and the smell of roasting beef was already permeating the air.

He mopped his brow, and backed away to the safety of the bar. The heat in the kitchen had made him itch, but the cool air soothed the burning, prickly sensation that was beginning to irritate him. He mopped the sweat away once more, but the itching increased. With some annoyance he ran his handkerchief under the cold tap and mopped again — this time the itching seemed to die down, and he promptly got busy restocking the bar. He didn't want to risk the slightest thing being at fault when the Licensed Vitctualler's arrived for lunch.

At twelve o' clock sharp, a mini-bus rolled to a halt, and a dozen or so smartly dressed gentlemen made their way into the Duck & Ferret for lunch. Kinsman straightened his tie and went forth to meet his public.

A shriek from the barmaid focussed all eyes on Kinsman's face. It was not a pretty sight: from hairline to collar it was a livid with weeping pustules that seemed to break out almost as they watched. His ears stood out like beacons, while his pale eyes looked most peculiar against the angry blotches. Suddenly aware of a strange sensation, he rubbed frantically, which only triggered off the awful itching, and 'arfa Kinsman was forced to retire to his room with the worst case of scald-head ever seen in the village.

The Licensed Vitctualler's, having taken one look at this awful spectre, had turned on their heels and left, vowing to find another venue — even if they had to settle for fish and chips. Words like 'disgraceful', 'revolting', and 'unhealthy' were overheard, and two days later a rather terse letter arrived announcing an impending visit to the Duck & Ferret by Environmental Health officials. The best laid plans of mice and men can always come unstuck, and a week later 'arfa Kinsman was last seen leaving in a taxi — a small removal van following behind — and leaving no forwarding address. His short reign at the Duck & Ferret had come to an untimely end — while his eczema lived on unchallenged — and impervious to anything the dermatologists prescribed.

As Pris later commented, he and the pustular postulant now didn't spoil a matching pair. Rupert heard the tale in silence but it was obvious that he was desperately trying not to laugh as he tacked up the horse for a morning ride out.

It wasn't until I was clearing out the usual debris that accumulates in farmhouse kitchens that I re-discovered the fetish that Rupert had found concealed in his saddle earlier in the year. It had been stuck on top of the dresser in a sealed glass jar so, in effect, the ill-wishing that had probably come with it was contained in a traditional 'witch bottle'. As it was impossible to determine the precise nature of the hex it was pointless attempting to return 'it' ... whatever 'it' was, and so it was best left alone and buried somewhere well away from the house and yard.

It was important that the witch bottle remained sealed ... a fact that had completely escaped one witch of our acquaintance. On removing a similar object from a victim's home, he had promptly taken it down to the canal and emptied the contents into the dark sluggish waters, and then chucked the bottle in after them! This meant that the hex was completely uncontained and uncontrollable and if he thought that stretch of the Trent & Mersey possessed the cleansing properties of 'clear, running water' then he needed to re-assess his magical training!

On a more personal level, I'd my own personal axe to grind over the pustular postulant. True, she'd tried to inveigle her way into both our Coven and our lives, but also had several attempts at trying her hand at seducing Rupert. I'd actually overheard a couple of the exchanges and my old Man had been positively rude to her but it didn't dampen her ardour — or her determination to be accepted into the Coven by fair means or foul. Thoughtfully, I weighed the witch bottle in my hand and visualised the spotty mess that was the pustular postulant's face.

Without further ado I dropped the jar into the old slurry pit. It briefly floated on top of the foul-smelling liquid, then the thin crust parted and the witch bottle disappeared from view with a highly appropriate burp. It was consigned to the murky depths of the slurry pit with a few well-chosen words of my own. Vengeance is mine, sayeth the Dame!

No matter how many so-called festivals are now included in the pagan calendar, for our ancestors there were only two important divisions in the year: summer and winter ... the seed-time and harvest ... the turning out of livestock and the bringing it back in again. These were the ancient divisions of the year in all parts of Britain although, because of the differences in regional climate and temperature, the festivals could be observed several weeks apart.

Summer would have been heralded by the flowering of the hawthorn and the sprouting of the spring grass; winter would have come when the last of the harvest was gathered in and the stock brought home for culling. All the hard work through the long summer months would be celebrated and nature's bounty acknowledged. There were times, of course, when the harvest was poor and there would have been little to celebrate ... even in our time there have been years when the harvest has failed.

But this year there were no such fears for the future and for the Coven there is no celebration more important than the Harvest Home. It is an occasion we share with our fellow coveners and those who work for us on the farm. It's often been observed that there have always been two religions in the British Isles: the doctrine of the church and the old, pre-Christian religion followed by those whose lives depended on the land. This is why the early church was forced to adopt many of the old indigenous traditions and bring them within the framework of the religious calendar.

Many of these old practices remained outside the parameters of the church, however, and still survive today in what has been called the 'rural underground'. A farmer can take all care and precaution humanly possible but still harbour the sure knowledge that he is powerless against the vagaries of Nature, should she decide to thwart him. Although these beliefs may appear out-dated and irrational to some who call themselves pagan, we nevertheless continue to observe them. For this reason the Man in Black will pour the last drop of the 'harvest cup' onto the ground as a libation.

Pris had volunteered to do the catering for our Harvest Home and so we decided to clear out the big barn for the occasion and hold a good old fashioned barn-dance to round off the evening. It was the very morning of the Harvest Home when we heard that Christine had eloped with a pharmaceutical salesman, who called regularly at the chemist shop where she worked. To me it sounded like something that only happened in a John Steinbeck novel but I hoped she'd be happier wherever she was than continuing to be used as a pawn in the religious chess-game played by her parents. At least the girl now had her freedom, but I still felt that Granny had been playing a dangerous game.

Gordon was making coffee in the tack room when I finally managed to catch him alone. "I hope you're not too upset by Christine running off and leaving you like that," I said.

"Well, she didn't exactly run off," he answered. "Her folks kept nagging me to leave the stables and get a better job and a couple of days ago, her father said he'd got me a job in a factory. I told him I wasn't working in any factory, and he said he wasn't having any stable lad marrying *his* daughter. I just said that was fine by me and if he was forcing me to chose between Christine and the horses, then there was no contest. This is where I belong and if they can't see that ... anyway, next thing I know she's gone."

"I'm glad if that's what you feel is right," I said, thinking that here was a chip off his old granddad's block and perhaps Rupert should let him have the old boy's cottage once the short-term lease was up.

"It's in my blood, Mrs P," he was saying. "This ... the stables ... the horses ... and the Coven. It's just that I'd never ... well, let's just say she glamoured me and I'm over it now. I think I'm going to be like granddad," he said, almost as if he were reading my thoughts. "You'll have to carry me out in my box."

Rooted and bound, rooted and bound ...

Later that evening the trestle tables were groaning with harvest fare and the fifty or so revellers were showing their appreciation by clearing their plates and not refusing a second-helping. A thick game soup with fresh crusty bread and butter was followed by a choice of baked ham and home-made pickles, or huge slices of May Butterworth's game pie, with baked potatoes and salad. May's apple and blackberry pies was served with lashings of fresh cream, followed by a selection of local cheeses. Pris had done us proud.

This was a 'working' meal and offered the type of food that would have been waiting in the farmhouse kitchen following a long day in the fields. Tonight, however, everyone was spruced up and taking full advantage of the copious supplies of beer, cider and robust red wine. At the end of the meal, before the tables were moved for dancing, Rupert proposed a toast to the bountiful harvest and was joined in a rousing rendering of *John Barleycorn, The Lincolnshire Poacher, John Peel* and *The Farmer's Boy*, all with varying degrees of inebriation.

Madeleine and Robert had flown back from Dubai, expressly to join the party; as had Richard and Philly, who had taken time off from their studies. Gordon's fling with Christine and his subsequent temporary job with an important race-horse trainer had given him a new-found confidence. He'd gone off a likeable lad and returned a handsome young man, who'd been surrounded by a bevy of local girls throughout the meal. *We have to let them go ... so that eventually they come back.*

A local folk-group provided the music and the evening was in full swing when Granny sidled up to me, having been allowed back from her brief exile now that Christine and 'arfa Kinsman had left the area.

"How did you do it?" she asked between sips of cider.

"Do what?"

"Prise the lad off that girl. I took care of her all right but he was a bit of a sticker. Thought for a time we'd lose him."

"Just a matter of knowing the right application," I replied in a non-committal way.

The old girl glanced at me sharply and I knew I'd hit a raw nerve. She obviously thought I'd not heard about her deliberately infecting 'arfa Kinsman with scald-head, but May Butterworth hadn't been slow in seeing an opportunity to pay Granny back for all the grievances that had piled up over the years. They might now be good pals on the surface but these old country women can harbour a grudge worse than any Borgia.

Granny had merely overlooked the obvious in her approach to the problem but it wouldn't hurt her to wonder about what kind of magic I'd used to bring things back under our control. She'd judged us all incapable of sorting out the problems and taken it upon herself to show us how things were done in the Old Ways. In doing so, she had broken a hundred-year old tradition of not going against the express order of the Man in Black, and if we *were* still operating under the laws of the Old Ways, she would have been strangled with her own cord!

Rooted and bound, rooted and bound ...

There was one last task to perform and this was to be a symbolic gesture of sowing wild-flower seeds in the grass margins. In the old days, the sowing of the corn was attended by all manner of rites and observations before the land was considered fit for drilling. In these times of modern agricultural methods many of these methods have fallen by the wayside but there are those that still endure. To test if the land is ready, the farmer simply walks across his fields and 'to feel it through his boots' as he takes up a handful of soil, in just the same way as they did back in the 16th-century.

Sound like superstitious nonsense? A 16th-century writer on agriculture named Fitzherbert wrote: *"Go upon the land that is ploughed and if it synge or crye or make any noise under thy fete, then it is to wet to sowe. And if it make no noyse and will bear thy horses, thanne sowe in the name of Godd."*

We decided to sow the wild-flower seeds as an offering after the Harvest Home simply because in the wild, the seeds were already in the ground, and many of them benefit from being frozen during the winter months as an aid to germination. Another old country belief is that all seed should be sown while the moon is waxing and harvested when the moon is waning.

The new moon was only two days away and it was on this late September night that Rupert and Adam made their way through the darkness of the yard to where an old hay turner partially concealed the fiddle drill. Rupert glanced at Adam and grinned — his teeth showing unnervingly white in the gloom. "Okay, which of us is going to make the biggest prat of ourselves then" he asked. Without hesitation Adam volunteered Rupert for the job of shouldering the strange instrument. Rupert chuckled good naturedly. "Suits me fine. It just means that you get to haul that bloody great bag of seed along while capering in an unmanly fashion behind me"

The two men guffawed like schoolboys, having fortified themselves for the ordeal with a hefty portion of *Grouse*. Then they both became serious. The same thought crossed both their minds as they shrugged out of their clothes and decided to cheat by putting boxers, socks and boots back on.

"It's all very well keeping the faith," muttered Adam, " but I for one don't want to find some bloody abandoned needle through my foot."

Rupert nodded. "Yup — common sense in all things these days, I'm afraid — besides we've got to have somewhere to keep the first aid flask."

Without another word he shouldered the cumbersome drill, and looked to see if Adam was ready. Adam hoisted the half sack and giving the 'thumbs up', they stepped out of the barn into the chill night air, glancing up at the moon. Light clouds scudded across her face, but it was otherwise clear, and with a sense of purpose the two men set off along the hedgerow. In the distance a dog barked, but apart from the slight swish of their own feet in the long headland grass, the night was calm and quiet.

Rupert began to work the drill, and soon fell into a rhythm that

Adam had no trouble in following. As the last sounds of civilisation fell away into the night, Adam began the old chant of the fields. The whirl of the drill strings was a two-time beat, and the two men fell easily into step with it, Adam maintaining the chant, while Rupert took up the chorus. In the damp night air, a steady spray of seed fell silently to earth, and the chant became more insistent.

To a casual onlooker the sight of two grown men in boxers and boots, pacing steadfastly through the darkness, while muttering some gibberish may have appeared more than mildly ridiculous. Especially as the arm-action required to work a fiddle drill bears an uncanny likeness to what Adam insisted on referring to as 'unnatural practices' and which never failed to inspire a great deal of mirth and ribald comments among those who witnessed it.

Granny had once muttered darkly at this childish humour and bit back saying, "Why the devil do you think it *is* used, you clowns!" which was quite a sobering thought.

Against the backdrop of owls hooting, and the odd scream of the fox, Adam and Rupert worked steadily round the boundary fields. The chanting became hypnotic and they walked on in a strange state of mind. The whirl of the drill, and the fall of the seed, created an eerie musical background to the old words of the charm. As they approached the almost total blackness of the top spinney, the spell was suddenly broken.

Rupert let out a howl as he lost his footing on the slope and skidded on the wet, churned up mud that formed the cows' favourite watering hole. Adam came to with a start just in time to see Rupert slithering down the embankment towards the stream — legs splayed out and the fiddle drill halfway over his head. His own whoop of laughter was cut short when his own feet shot out from under him, and in spite of a valiant effort, he too went sprawling in the mud. Face down and travelling at what felt like warp speed, he cannoned into Rupert, knocking the drill out of his hands. The two men just gave in and rolled about, helpless with laughter.

"Well, that's one way of honouring the age old custom of testing the earth to see if it's ready for sowing," said Adam dryly, referring to the practice of testing the warmth of the earth through the most sensitive part of the anatomy. Suddenly, it dawned on them that the water was actually *very* cold — and what they were sitting in wasn't simply mud.

"My God you stink!" roared Rupert, to which Adam replied, "Yeah, well, they always reckon that foxes smell their own first."

The banter went on as they hauled themselves up and scrambled up the banking. Filthy, smelly and decidedly dishevelled, they examined the drill. "Thank the gods there's no harm done," Rupert commented.

Adam looked ruefully at the depleted seed bag. "I think the old spinney's got a bit more than its fair share, but c'mon, there's still enough here to see us round."

Rupert shielded his eyes in a mock gesture. "Onwards and upwards then ... c'mon soldier let's get finished, I'm frozen stiff."

As they were about to set off Adam let out a yell. "Damn! Where's the flask?" The thought of his beloved hip-flask basking in the stream was too much to contemplate. Without thinking he plunged back down the embankment and began grovelling about in the dark. Suddenly there was a loud whoop of success. "Got it! Give us a hand up or I'll drink it all myself."

That threat alone was an inspiration in itself; Rupert held out a muddy hand and hauled Adam back up the banking. Once on terra firma again they wasted no time in knocking back the contents of the flask. The hypnotic mood had been broken, but as the drill and themselves were still in one piece they decided to press on and finish the job.

"In for a penny — in for a pound," Rupert grunted, as he shouldered the drill and struck out again along the hedge.

Adam topped the drill-bag up again and nodded. "What is it that these modern pagans say about rituals of love and laughter? Well, the Old Bugger is certainly having a laugh at us tonight."

Rupert grinned as he replied. "We must look a bonny pair, let's press on before dawn breaks and someone catches us looking like this." Resolutely they set off again: after a few minutes they fell back into step, and the chanting continued — albeit a bit more quietly than before.

It was a tired, cold, hungry and footsore pair that crept into the yard just as the light was breaking towards the east. Moving stealthily, Rupert pressed the latch on the old kitchen door, and opened it very slowly without a creak.

"Thank goodness the Aga's still going full pelt, I'm frozen." I heard him whisper as he crept across the kitchen. He let Adam close the door and just as he set off towards the welcoming warmth, the overhead lights snapped on.

"Hold it right there!" said Pris. The sight that met our eyes was one that we would never forget and, thanks to a disposable camera, it was one that neither Rupert nor Adam would ever be allowed to. "Out to the trough, *right now,*" she bellowed. "If you two think for one moment that you're skulking in here smelling like that, you've got another think coming."

Without a word of retaliation the two men turned and sheepishly made for the door. The sight of the two behinds, clad in muddy, wet boxer shorts that drooped and slapped against two small cold bottoms sent us both over the edge. Weak with laughing, but still sharp enough to spot the moment, I made sure the camera flashed again, and the men bolted for the safety of the yard to undergo further humiliation.

"Do we call this 'one for posterity'?" howled Priss, but the best was yet to come.

Our lurcher, woken by the noise, had come out to see what all the fuss was about and with a quizzical look, plonked his haunches down on the cobbles to watch. Now in his time he had enjoyed rolling in just about every revolting concoction available to a dog. From dead sheep to fox droppings, he had wriggled with delight in them all — only to have to suffer the discomfort of being hosed down before being allowed back in the house. Hosed down, in fact, at the side of the very same trough that the two men now dithered beside. He licked his lips and settled down to watch.

Without further ado, Pris turned on the hose and the two men reluctantly struggled with caked-on mud and streaks of 'nervous cow'. Dripping from head to foot, boxer shorts clinging pitifully to their legs, we eventually took pity on them.

"Oh enough, I can't stand to see a grown man suffer," I giggled.

"Oh, I can," Pris replied, " I haven't laughed so much since Walter Middleton tried to take that old gelding of his wife's hunting. It must have galloped four miles with him — trouble was it was *away* from the field and then came home without him, having deposited the old boy in a slurry pit."

Her reminiscing was broken by Rupert. "I'm frozen stiff and I have every intention of entering my own home right now." He strode haughtily away towards the kitchen. Adam only hesitated for a second before bolting after him

Pris and I exchanged sidelong grins and winked. "Okay boys, a joke's a joke but you two are cold. The water's piping hot, so dash off and have a shower before you catch your deaths."

"We'll get on with breakfast," I added, "and we'll ask them how they got in that state later."

It might not have been the most sophisticated ritual in the history of Craft but it was one in time honoured tradition. Pris and I had performed a similar women's rite during the previous year, and it says a lot for our menfolk that they were willing to subject themselves to the cold and humiliation that only the Old Ones can inflict on us when they wish to amuse themselves at our expense. Few people today give them the opportunity since most contemporary rituals are conducted behind closed doors.

All Hallows

The night was clear and sharp.   Immediately overhead the Milky Way stretched from the eastern to the western horizon and the huge full moon hung low and orange in the south. This was a very special occasion since it marked not only our All Hallows gathering but was also a 'blue moon' - when there are two full moons in a calendar month.   And, with the coming of winter, we could see at last the return of the Hunter, followed by the Dog Star, climbing in the south-east.

It was to be a full Coven meeting — all those who had undergone Initiation and, for the first time in many years, included Granny. She'd muttered something about "seeing if Old Joe were alright" and wasn't going to be put off by the fact that it would mean walking across several fields, climbing stiles and negotiating stepping stones across a small stream. It was on the way home from this site that Pris had encountered the bull at last Winter Solstice but this time Joseph was safely penned back at the farm.

Another year was over and we'd managed to come through it reasonably unscathed, although Rupert admitted that he was becoming more and more jaded by Craft with each passing year. He still enjoyed working with Pris and Adam, simply because we know each other so well, but a full Coven gathering was something he could well live without — especially as Granny was coming too!

"It will sound like a bloody Salvation Army band, traipsing across those fields," he grumbled. "And some idiot is sure to fall in the stream ... And what does that silly old fool want to come for, anyway? She's just out to cause trouble, I know it. Probably because you outsmarted her over Gordon ... She'll be up to her old tricks, you mark my words."

"We can hardly refuse her under the circumstances," I replied, mentally ticking off who would be coming to the gathering.

Apart from myself and Rupert, there would be Pris and Adam, Gerry and Guy, Madelaine and Robert, Gordon and Granny, which made ten in all. With a place laid for the 'dumb supper', we were only two short of a traditional Coven — but it was enough. It would have been nice to include Philly and Richard (who weren't old enough to take Initiation) and Abi and Carole (who were only beginners) but Coven rules are there to be observed, not broken.

By way of a compromise, Rupert had been up to the site earlier that afternoon and collected enough firewood to see us through the long night. He had also lugged Pris's huge cauldron containing a rich beef stew since one vessel large enough to feel 10 hungry witches would have taken some carrying, and none of us were getting any younger. The rest would have to manage carrying the bread and wine between them, he said.

By the time we'd all arrived at the working site, the fire was glowing and the cauldron bubbling away, wafting the smell of stew out under the trees. Drawing on his woodman's skills, Rupert had set the fire-pit earlier and the food would be ready for when the ritual ended. Although it wasn't a cold night, the welcoming glow from the fire meant that we could all robe in comfort, instead of shivering behind the bushes. Usually *someone* falls over when hopping from one leg to another, trying to remove boots under the cover of darkness ... that is, if they haven't gone in the stream first.

"What do you reckon Granny's up to?" whispered Pris as she pulled on her robe.

"Rupert reckons she's only here to cause trouble," I answered softly, so as not to be overheard.

"She wouldn't dare," said Pris. "Not here, not tonight. She's too much respect for the Old Ways, even if she hasn't any for its officers."

"Well, brace yourself Myrtle," I replied, "we'll find out soon enough."

One by one, ten cowled figures formed the Circle around the fire, each standing with their heads bowed, hands folded inside the sleeves of their robes. This was the quiet-time needed to separate the mundane from the spiritual, and at this point all tom-foolery ceased. Each person drawing on the teaching of the Old Ways according to their own individual lights.

Everyone has their own way of preparing themselves for Circle and I glanced around at my fellow coveners, wondering what was going through their minds at this precise moment in time. Immediately opposite me stood Gordon, his handsome features accentuated by the flickering firelight under the shadow of the cowl. Was he thinking about Christine, or had he put all that aside now that he knew where he belonged. And Granny. Was she thinking about her youth when she and Old Joe had their little fling?

It was a glorious night and if we'd have tried to create a blueprint for the perfect conditions for an outdoor ritual, this could not have been bettered. The moon was veiled by a slight haze, which meant the woods were bathed in a muted light as we waited for the signs that we were welcome. One by one they came. One by one those standing at the Quarters acknowledged the acceptance and the rite was allowed to begin. The Horned Keeper of the woods and dales was being summoned ...

It seems like a contradiction in terms to say that the ritual was carefully choreographed and yet each individual acted according to the spontaneous impulses of his or her nature. The power was built and the Circle enhanced: outside a dog fox called to the vixen, while overhead owls hunted and called. Pacing the Circle, the Old Words rose and fell in a rhythmic chant, we all began to feel the razor-edge of the psychic cold enveloping the sacred space.

The power was building and flowing in outward-circling spirals, as the gaps between the trees glowed with a faint blue, luminous light. On the periphery of my vision I could make out a vaporous, cowled figure pacing on the outside of the Circle in unison with our own rhythmic steps. One by one the Coven members noticed it and slowly all movement ceased as we silently welcomed our visitor — whoever it may be.

As the others admitted later, it was probably the most exhilarating experience any of us had ever had during an All Hallows ritual. We pay homage to our ancestors but rarely do we get the opportunity to meet them cowl to cowl, as it were. The previous year Granny had told us of the war-time ritual that had gone so horribly wrong, and that she had never since managed to make contact with anything ever again during group work. Now, on the very night she was with us for the first in years, it had happened again.

Pris must have been thinking about the same thing, because at that moment we both glanced at Granny. Under the shadow of her hood, tears were streaming down her cheeks but the look of rapt wonder was a sight we'd never seen before on the old witch's face. Unconsciously she wiped her nose on her sleeve but never took her eyes from the Old One as she sunk to the knees on the hard ground.

Coarse Witchcraft 3: Cold Comfort Coven is currently in preparation and this will be the last in the series as there have been some drastic changes within the Coven.

Recommended Reading:

13 Moons, Fiona Walker Craven (ignotus)
The Country Book of the Year,
Dennis L Furnell (David & Charles)
Country Seasons, Philip Clucas (Windward)
From Lark Rise to Candleford, Flora Thompson (OUP)
Root & Branch: British Magical Tree Lore,
Paul Harriss & Mélusine Draco (ignotus)
The Witch's Treasury of the Countryside,
Paul Harriss & Mélusine Draco (ignotus)

Other titles from members of the Coven:

Coarse Witchcraft: Coven Working

A Witch's Treasury of Hearth & Garden

White Horse: Equine Magical Lore

Coming soon

Aubry's Dog: Canine Magical Lore

Coarse Witchcraft: Cold Comfort Coven

Wood Craft

Field Craft

Black Thorn, White Thorn

Further titles available at discount prices from The Hemlock Club

See details of our current and forthcoming titles by sending SAE to the address below or log on to our website at www.ignotuspress.com Titles currently include:

13 Moons by Fiona Walker-Craven
Coarse Witchcraft: Craft Working by Rupert & Gabrielle Percy
Coven of the Scales by Bob Clay-Egerton
Coven Working by Carrie West & Philip Wright
Death & the Pagan by Phillip Wright & Carrie West
The Egyptian Book of Days by Mélusine Draco
The Egyptian Book of Nights by Mélusine Draco
High Rise Witch by Fiona Walker-Craven
The Hollow Tree by Mélusine Draco
The Inner Guide to Egypt by Alan Richardson & Billie Walker John
Irish Witchcraft by St John D Seymour
Liber Ægyptius by Mélusine Draco
Malleus Satani—The Hammer of Satan by Suzanne Ruthven
The Odd Life & Inner Work of W G Gray
                    by Alan Richardson & Marcus Claridge
Rites of Shadow by E A St George
Root & Branch: British Magical Tree Lore
                    by Paul Harriss & Mélusine Draco
Sea Witch, Paul Holman
The Setian by Billie Walker-John
The Thelemic Handbook by Mélusine Draco
What You Call Time by Suzanne Ruthven
White Horse: Equine Magical Lore by Rupert Percy
A Witch's Treasury of the Countryside
                    by Paul Harriss & Mélusine Draco
A Witch's Treasury for Hearth & Garden by Gabrielle Sidonie

ignotus press is an independent publisher whose authors are all genuine magical practitioners, willing to answers questions on any subjects mentioned in their books.

ignotus press, BCM-Writer, London WC1N 3XX